MEDEIA SHARIF

Evernight Teen ®

www.evernightteen.com

A LOVE THAT DISTURBS

Copyright© 2016

Medeia Sharif

ISBN: 978-1-77233-892-8

Cover Artist: Jay Aheer

Editor: Jessica Ruth

ALL RIGHTS RESERVED

MEDEIA SHARIF

DEDICATION

For DH

MEDEIA SHARIF

A LOVE THAT DISTURBS

Medeia Sharif

Copyright © 2016

Chapter One

November 10, 2014
7:32 a.m.

"First period started a few minutes ago. I'll write you a late pass."

Haydee nodded and gulped. She was going to finish her education in a regular school, which wasn't normal for her. She had been in an alternative school for the first three years of high school. Now it was the second quarter of her senior year. Because of good behavior, she was in her "home" school, based on the boundaries of her residence. This was the school she should have been in after middle school, before her life spiraled out of control. Haydee wished Aunt Dayana had stuck around. Her aunt had driven her here and finished registering her, but she'd had to leave to drop her own children at their schools. Haydee was by herself. She'd been aware of this for years, but she still wished someone would be at her side. Alone, she made bad decisions and fell into the hands of the wrong people. She didn't mean to, but it happened. As she sat in front of the woman's desk, she vowed she'd be a loner in this new environment, so she

7

wouldn't get into any trouble.

The counselor smiled. She was a petite, middle-aged blonde with too many teeth. The woman glanced from her eyes to the side of her face, back and forth, the eye movements real obvious. Haydee knew why. She had a faint black eye on the left side of her face. Because of the medium tone of her skin, when people noticed the bruise, she told them it was a birthmark.

"If you have any problems, my door is always open," Ms. Freeman said.

She was too perky for this time of day and when Haydee was feeling no confidence for her *new beginning* at this school. Squirming on the hard plastic seat, she looked down at her tattooed thigh, at the jaguar leaping from her flesh. On the other leg, from ankle to knee, was a vine of flowers. The tattoos were meaningless. She got them at a time when she thought they were cool, because all her friends—or *former associates* as she should call them, because they had never been real friends—were getting them, too. She shouldn't have worn khaki uniform shorts and could've worn the pants instead. Feeling too exposed, she tugged on her sleeves. At least the hoodie she was wearing over the navy blue polo shirt covered her tattooed arms.

Haydee took the yellow pass from the counselor. In her other sweaty hand was her schedule. Sweat also dotted her brow, even though the school hallways were freezing. Instead of going directly to her first class, which was English, she went to the bathroom and splashed cold water on her face. Her tattooed hands, which had a skull on the right hand beneath her thumb and the letters $H S Q$ $U A D$ on the fingers of her left hand—remnants of her brief time in a gang—went up and down, from the faucet to her face. She didn't have any makeup on, when normally she wore it. She wasn't thinking about looking pretty in the morning, but she had to look pretty at night, for the job she didn't want to do. The water across her face felt good. She even cupped her hands and drank some of it. When she lifted her head, she blinked as water dripped on her hoodie, and she fumbled for the closest towel dispenser only to find that it was empty.

The door swooshed open and the giggling of girls penetrated the quiet space. Haydee froze. Her body tensed even though she wasn't at work, where she always had to argue with someone and risk being beaten. She was in a school … but she had been beaten up a few times at school, too.

"Here," someone said. The voice was soft and gentle. Haydee faced the sink, with her eyes partially closed as water continued to drip down her face, when a stranger brushed against her. The person placed towels into her wet hands. When Haydee grabbed them, by accident she pinched the girl's hands and wrists.

"Thank you," Haydee mumbled against the towels. When she pulled the towels off, she was looking directly at someone's oval face. The girl was beautiful. Her dark brows and long lashes were striking, like black ink drawn on her face by an artist. Her lips were pink, but it didn't look like she wore any lipstick. Around her head was a floral, printed scarf with pink flowers and bright green leaves. Her hands, which Haydee had awkwardly squeezed when handling the towels, had long, thin fingers and neat nails.

Next to the girl were three others—one who was very pale with a hawkish nose, another light-skinned, and another with dusky skin. Only the hawkish one had her long, frizzy hair loose. Haydee wondered where they all were from, since it was rare to see girls wearing scarves in school—thinking about it, she had never seen classmates wear them and had only spotted a few women at the mall who dressed like that. Were they Hindu? Buddhist? Haydee felt like a dunce … no, they were Muslim. She had seen women wearing scarves like that on the news.

"Hold our cameras for us," someone told the nice girl. They handed her three camera cases, and the girl looped them around one arm.

"Your schedule is wet," the nice girl said. The three other girls were using the stalls, so Haydee was alone with her.

"Oh no," Haydee said, bending down to pick it off the floor. She folded the damp paper and put it into her pocket before she damaged it some more.

"Are you new?" the girl asked. "I'm Maysa."

"I'm Haydee. Yeah, I'm new."

Maysa smiled. Her teeth were perfect and her full lips stretched. Haydee didn't know if she should be talking to her. Maysa looked too clean-cut. She doubted Maysa and the girls she was with had tattoos. They opted for the khaki pants instead of shorts, wore long sleeves, and they were the chattering, innocent types. Even behind the stalls, the girls talked to each other about everyday things.

"Did you do Mr. Stahl's homework?"

"Yes, of course I did."

"Can I copy?"

"Can I borrow your mascara?"

They even laughed amid the noise of pee dropping into the water. They flushed seconds apart and exited the stalls in unison, crowding around Haydee and Maysa to wash their hands. Haydee stepped to the side, away from the mirror and sinks, to make room for the group of friends. "We're not skipping," Maysa explained. "We're on the yearbook committee and we're going around taking pictures." She yanked up a laminated press pass of sorts that hung from her neck, with her name underneath the label *YEARBOOK*. Maysa Mazari. Such an exotic name, a beautiful name for a beautiful girl.

Maysa's friends took their camera bags from her. "It was nice meeting you," she said. "Everyone, this is Haydee. She's new to the school. This is Aamal, Ruhat, and Imani."

Haydee paid attention during this introduction. Aamal was the pale covered one, Imani was the dark covered one, and Ruhat was the uncovered one. Aamal sneered at her, while the other two wore neutral expressions. Haydee felt dirty next to them since they dressed modestly and were in the yearbook class. Only goody-goody girls were involved with that. Those girls were smart, pristine, and the opposite of what she was. They were also *involved*, when she had never been in a club or committee in her life at a time when most of her classmates fretted about what to add on their college applications. Haydee wasn't even sure yet if she was going to college.

"Well, bye," Maysa said. "Maybe I'll see you later if we have any classes together. Since you came this time of the year, it's too late to take senior pictures, so you won't be in that section of the yearbook, but you might show up in the random school pics we all take."

The girls left and Haydee let out a long sigh. That was awkward, at least the part when Maysa's friends were obviously uninterested in her, but Maysa was nice. Haydee wondered what Maysa would look like without the scarf on her head. Was her hair long or short? Curly or straight? Based on her eyebrows, it was probably dark, but maybe it had red highlights.

Not that it mattered. Nice or not, girls like Maysa didn't hang out with people like her. Haydee had no time for friends anyway, which suited her fine—anyone who found out what she had done and what she was currently doing to survive would be disgusted.

Chapter Two

November 10, 2014
7:40 a.m.

Maysa walked behind her friends. They were buzzing about Haydee, the new girl they had just met in the bathroom. Even though it was a brief meeting, they all had opinions on her.

"If she's coming this time of year, it's for one of two reasons," Aamal said. "She either moved or was kicked out of her school."

"She could be from one of those schools for juvenile delinquents," Ruhat said. "We see them here sometimes. Remember last year how we found out that boy had stabbed his father? We were like, *what's he doing here?*"

Imani stayed quiet. Not because she was the quiet type, but because she wasn't the type to say anything mean about others. Out of their group of friends, Imani was the one Maysa was closest to. They were more alike, whereas Ruhat and Aamal had more in common, although Aamal stood out the most.

"Just stay the hell away from her and she won't cause any problems for us," Aamal said. "That's probably the last time we'll see her."

Maysa reached for her vibrating phone, which snagged on the edge of her pocket. The girls walking in front of her were her only friends, so she wondered who was contacting her. The distance between them increased as Maysa stood in one spot to wrestle the phone out of her pocket. Her friends didn't notice that she wasn't with them. Aamal's covered head moved side to side as she spoke, while Imani's *hijab* had a loose end that swayed

13

with her movements and lifted when a gust from an air conditioning vent hit it. Her friends turned a corner and disappeared. Maysa would catch up with them once she read the text message she'd just received. It was from her mother.

The message contained a screen capture showing pictures of three boys from her mother's Facebook account. Along with the pictures was a message: **Look at how Nazneen's sons have grown! All around your age. :)**

Nazneen was a family friend, someone who lived hours from them in another part of Florida. Maysa only recalled meeting her two or three times, the last time being when her sons were in middle school. They had been annoying, pulling her hair or excluding her from their backyard games. She didn't even recall their names. They were all brown and Pakistani like she was, and back then immature. It was obvious they had grown, with trimmed facial hair and sharp features. All a year apart from each other, they were good-looking, but Maysa didn't want them. In the past few months, Maysa's mother had mentioned *arranged marriage* and all the *eligible Pakistani boys* in their area. Maysa didn't want that life. She wanted to choose who to be with. She wanted to fall in love, just like in her favorite movies. There was an ache to mimic *Titanic*, to have that sweeping love she saw between Jack and Rose … not what her mother had in mind for her, a cold meeting between her and a boy to see if they were *compatible* enough to marry each other.

Maysa had already told her mother that she didn't like the idea and that she didn't want her parents to make such a big decision like this for her. **No thanks**, she texted.

You will change your mind, her mom texted back.

Maysa gritted her teeth. Her mother was always saying things like that—she knew what was best for her daughter, that Maysa was being stubborn and would change her mind, and she was being defiant. Why was wanting to be happy and independent such a bad thing in her mother's eyes?

Imani peered out from the corner they had turned. "Are you coming?" she asked.

"I'll be right there. I was reading a text."

"We split up," Imani said, walking toward her with her camera bag in hand. "Aamal is doing science, and she said I'm doing math, Ruhat is doing electives, and you can take pictures of the English classes."

Maysa hadn't realized that while she'd held the phone in one hand, she had twisted and squeezed the strap of the camera bag in the other between sweaty fingers. After Imani glanced down at her hands, she loosened her hold on the camera bag. "I'll go now."

She walked with Imani to the end of the hallway and they parted ways. Maysa frowned as she thought about her mother's disturbing text message. Once she knocked on the door of an English class, opened it, and saw who was there, her face lit up into a smile. She wasn't quite sure why she was pleased. Maybe it was the prospect of making a new friend, even though her current friends didn't like this person at all. Sitting in the back of the classroom was Haydee, who looked up when the door squeaked wide open.

Chapter Three

November 10, 2014
7:40 a.m.

As she lingered in the bathroom, when she should have been heading to the first class on her newly printed schedule, her phone vibrated. It was as if *he* could read her thoughts from far away. She took the phone out of her back pocket. Spidery cracks webbed all over the face of it, but it was all she had for communication for now. Because the phone was lit up, the cracks weren't as pronounced. *RAFE*, the caller ID read. Then it went to voicemail. Haydee shivered. She knew firsthand what he was capable of. She patted the bruise on her face and winced. Deep in the skin, the pain he had inflicted lingered.

"Shit," she said out loud, her voice echoing in the empty bathroom. She had that same feeling she'd experienced in the counselor's office: she wished she weren't alone. She thought about her aunt again, who owned a laundry service a few blocks away. Her old friends … what friends? Some of them had been high or drunk together, so did that count as friendship? Many of them had moved and some were in prison. No, she had no friends.

Haydee wished Maysa were with her, filling her with friendly banter and telling her about the school—which teachers were easy, which were hard, and what was good to eat in the cafeteria—but that was silly. She had just met her. She felt like a dude who thought the wrong things just because a girl smiled at him. That wasn't a come-on of any sort. Maysa was friendly, not friends material.

Haydee put the phone on the sink's counter with shaking hands. She didn't want to hear Rafe's voice. She'd ignore him. Although, when she had ignored him in the past he'd always come for her, hounding her through her phone or showing up where he knew she would be. Pimps didn't easily let go of their hoes.

She studied her reflection. Tears sprouted in her eyes. Being extremely tardy to her first period wouldn't look good, so she breathed deeply and pulled her long hair into a bun. She dug around in her book bag, spilling some hot chips out of a bag and dirtying a new notebook with their orange crumbs, until she found a blue pen and added ten minutes to the time Ms. Freeman had put on the pass. She couldn't get into trouble at school on her first day here. Even though she was used to alternative schools and juvie, she wanted to stay here, in this normal school. She had to blend in and be like everyone else.

Her phone vibrated again. **I know you there**, Rafe texted. **Text me when you can. Lunch time? We gotta discuss tonight.**

Haydee wondered how many johns he had found for tonight. Old ones? Smelly ones? Ones who hated wearing condoms? Haydee shivered again as she thought about what she had seen, what she had done at the request of these men.

After her father left, she'd thought the gang would keep her safe, which wasn't the case since bad things had kept coming her way. A week after her mom was arrested for grand theft, she turned her first trick. She wished Aunt Dayana had taken custody of her sooner. After living with her aunt, she was no longer involved with the gang, but Rafe was another matter. Anytime she seemed to rebel, he held her in check. Lately she had a burning desire to lead a clean life, but was that even possible after all she had done?

At least Rafe wouldn't bother her for a few hours. He knew it was her first day in a new school. Haydee blew her nose, wiped her eyes, and left the bathroom. She walked into first period English and handed the teacher the pass. Students stared. A few had tattoos peeking from the edges of sleeves and shorts, but nothing like what she had. She felt like the Tattooed Woman and avoided staring back at them. She wasn't in alternative school anymore, where most students had a nasty attitude about anything related to academics. The students in front of her had their books open and had been reading and writing before she'd walked in. They weren't looking to fight her and she wasn't going to fight them.

"Let me write your name down," the teacher said. "I'll make a folder for your work. How do you say your name? Heidi?"

"No, it's Hay-dee," she corrected Ms. Tookes. "Haydee Gomez."

Ms. Tookes wrote her name on a notepad and nodded toward an empty desk, so Haydee sat down in a seat in the back with a textbook. The assignment was on the board, but Haydee had trouble seeing. She had lost or broken so many of her eyeglasses in the past that she'd stopped wearing them. She was slightly nearsighted and lived with her blurry vision just fine. Tomorrow she'd come to class on time and get a seat in the front.

She continued to receive some stares, but then students went back to work.

Feeling like she was on display, Haydee twirled the drawstrings of her hoodie, chewed the inside of her mouth, and smoothed down the baby hairs on her forehead. The door opened and she was grateful for another distraction. It was Maysa, her pink-and-green silk scarf glistening under the fluorescent lights. Haydee's vision sharpened, as if she could see Maysa clearly, while everything around her was fuzzy. Maysa caught Haydee's gaze and smiled before turning to Ms. Tookes. "May I take a few pictures of the students working?"

The teacher smiled back. "Take all the pictures you want."

Maysa had a sunny, innocent demeanor. Haydee wondered what it would be like to have her life. She must have two parents taking care of her. She probably had brothers and sisters who were as nice as she was. Her parents were strict, if she had to cover her head like that, but they most likely were loving. Haydee's curiosity intensified. She needed to know more about Maysa, who was walking to the back of the room where she was.

"Can I take a picture of you reading the textbook?" Maysa asked.

"Sure." Anything. She wanted to please this girl. Haydee opened to a random page. It was a Shakespearean sonnet, which was like another language to her. She liked to read, but not classic works. She enjoyed romance books and read any that she could get her hands on. They helped her escape from her own reality by taking her someplace else for a few hours.

Flashes sparked as Maysa took a few shots of Haydee. "You're very photogenic."

"Really?" Haydee looked up. "Let me see."

Maysa neared her and held the back of the camera to Haydee's face. Looking at the screen, Haydee saw she didn't look too bad. Her bun was messy in a stylish way, and her head was tilted down to her book. Her cheekbones were sharp, and her right side was on display—not the left one with the black eye. "It's a nice shot."

Maysa smiled, and Haydee blinked, not knowing what else to say or do. She wanted to keep Maysa talking so that she wouldn't leave right away. Because of the picture taking, a few other students had started talking and sneaked looks at the two of them. Haydee knew they must seem like an odd pair interacting with each other. Maysa showed her the next few pictures, at different angles. "I have to go now and get to the next classroom," she said.

"Oh, all right." Her gaze was riveted to Maysa's slender form as she walked out the door.

Haydee's phone vibrated again. When the teacher wasn't looking, she slid it out of her pocket.

Got a nice dress for you tonight
Come to my place later so you can try it on
Red, your perfect color

And just like that, the moment was ruined. She shoved her phone back into her pocket. Like she needed another reminder of everything that was wrong in her life. She gritted her teeth and made fists, then forced herself to loosen her hands. She didn't want to think about Rafe anymore, but how could she not? He was like a virus in her system and she couldn't get rid of him. She admitted that he took care of her: he beat up johns who mistreated her, handed over any money he promised her, and challenged anyone who bothered her on the rough streets of Miami.

If it hadn't been for Rafe, she might have been dead at one point, because one of the johns locked her in a bathroom, threatening to kill her later, and he took care of the situation. There were still the issues of earning money and a degree of safety, but surely she could find another line of work. How would she tell Rafe that she wanted out without having his temper explode? She had seen him cut a man's face with a razor. Would he do the same to her?

Chapter Four

November 20, 2014
6:00 a.m.

Maysa sat on her bed, waiting for her mother to be done in the bathroom. There was a second bathroom inside the master bedroom, but her father was using it. They were washing up for the pre-dawn morning prayer, *Fajr*. Maysa stretched her legs and clasped her hands together. She yawned. After prayer, she would have to get dressed for school.

Her little sister, Sanaa, was seven-years-old. She memorized the prayers but didn't pray, yet. It was just Maysa and her parents in the family room, facing Mecca as they genuflected. Maysa moved in slow motion, a second or two behind everyone else's movements. She was tired. All night she had studied, then edited pictures for the yearbook. There was also something else she had been doing that she would never tell anyone about, because she found it confusing—she had been studying yearbook pictures of Haydee.

Maysa rolled up her prayer rug. Her tall, lean, and dark father stifled a yawn. Her mother, who was short, thick, and pale, did the same. They would head out soon as well. They owned a few gas stations, with various cousins and family friends behind the counter, which seemed so typical for a Pakistani couple to do. Many family friends owned corner stores, but gas stations were a close second. It didn't seem like an interesting or exciting line of work, but Maysa wasn't going to complain since she knew college would be paid for and that she'd be under no financial debt.

"I'm going to get ready for school," Maysa said.

"Did you do your homework?" her father asked.

"Yes."

"You didn't show it to me."

Maysa chewed the inside of her cheek. She'd stopped showing him her homework last year because that seemed like such a babyish thing to do. Little kids had their homework checked by their parents.

"Remember how you received a *B* last quarter in math?"

How could she forget? Her parents were always throwing that in her face. They expected straight *A*'s from her. Anything less was failing. The pressure from them was an omnipresence always breathing down her back.

After a brief lecture on grades, college, and how hard real life was, her father stopped speaking. Even though his lectures irritated her, she preferred them to her mother showing her pictures of Pakistani bachelors who were husband material. Maysa left the family room on socked feet. All of their shoes were on a shoe rack in the living room. Her father didn't allow their family or any guests to wear shoes indoors because that was unclean. For a time, when Maysa was a child, they would leave their shoes on the porch but then neighborhood kids stole them. The shoe rack was now indoors.

Maysa closed her bedroom door and sat at her computer. She opened her flash drive, where the yearbook photos were. Amid the schoolwork folders was a separate folder labeled *Haydee*.

She clicked on one of the photos she had taken on Haydee's first day in school. The girl was beautiful. She and Maysa both had an olive undertone to their skin, although Haydee was lighter. Their eyes were different, because Haydee had hazel ones with a green ring surrounded by brown, and Maysa's were dark brown.

They also had a different build. Maysa was thinner, while Haydee had curves. There were more pictures. Maysa shared only one class with Haydee, AP chemistry. She had taken a few pictures of her there, too. In one of them Haydee smiled, which transformed her face. Her eyes crinkled and her straight teeth flashed when her pouty lips spread wide across her face.

Smiles were rare from Haydee, though. There was something sad about her—something around the eyes, and that dark bruise or birthmark on the left side of her face. She was quiet in class, always with her phone out to check messages. Who was sending her those messages? Haydee had not made one friend in the week and a half she had been at school. Maysa figured it was friends from her old school contacting her. She wanted to reach out, but her friends were a barrier. They didn't want Haydee anywhere near them.

****

8:00 a.m.

They were outside of their yearbook class, decorating for the annual Thanksgiving door project. The winning first period class would receive a donut party. It seemed like kid stuff, but some teachers were competitive about it. Ms. Montes chose Maysa, Aamal, Imani, and Ruhat to decorate the door. They were the only ones who seemed interested. There was barely a sound coming from the other side of the door because students were on computers, creating layouts, and typing captions or in the hallways looking for picture-taking opportunities.

"The girl looks dirty," Aamal said as she cut brown tissue paper.

"Ugh, I know," Ruhat said. She twisted her frizzy hair into a bun at the nape of her neck. She sniffled, rubbing her sharp nose with a finger. "I can't believe she asked us for help in chemistry yesterday. I pretended I didn't know anything."

"She looks like a walking STD," Imani joined in, which wasn't like her. "I also pretended I didn't know anything."

Except for Maysa, who was staying quiet, the girls were badmouthing Haydee for the second time since the girl's arrival. Aamal and Imani were covered like Maysa was, and both wore bright, colorful scarves, which Maysa also favored. Only Ruhat didn't wear *hijab*, because that wasn't what women did in her household. Ruhat's parents were Iraqi. Aamal's were Syrian, while Imani's were Pakistani. Maysa was closest to Imani because of this connection. Their parents were friends who had known each other in Lahore, and Imani was the sweetest girl in the group, even though she wasn't saying anything nice about Haydee at the moment. Sure Haydee had tattoos, was quiet, and was a loner, but those qualities weren't a crime. Haydee had approached them yesterday in chemistry because she was missing some notes, and when her friends were busy cleaning their lab area, Maysa had lent them to her.

"I'm sure none of you would be friends with that girl," Aamal said, directing her gaze at Maysa.

"I want nothing to do with her," Ruhat said.

"Me neither." Imani shook her head.

Maysa wouldn't say anything, and Aamal continued staring at her. Did she sense that Maysa was taking an interest in the girl? She had that creepy feeling that Aamal could read her thoughts or somehow knew she had been admiring pictures of Haydee. Standing behind Aamal was Imani, who flared her nostrils and frowned to imitate and mock Aamal's sour face. Maysa bit her lip so she wouldn't laugh aloud. Aamal turned around but didn't catch anything since Imani bent down to pick up a roll of tissue paper.

"Hand me some orange tissue paper," Aamal snapped. No matter what she said or did, her features looked like they were twisted in a perpetual sneer. She had flared nostrils and a corner of her lip always turned up. Even Maysa's mom said that Aamal would be pretty if she didn't always look like she was sucking on a lemon.

"Here it is." Imani offered her the roll of paper.

"I need scissors." Ruhat reached for a pair from a plastic bin of supplies their teacher had lent them.

"I need help on my math homework," Aamal said. "Who can I copy off of?"

Maysa's throat closed in discomfort. Aamal was always copying off others—particularly her, since she had the highest math scores in the bunch. Imani must have sensed Maysa's feelings, because she opened her mouth first. "You can copy off me."

"Thank you, friend." Aamal smiled, which only brightened her face a little bit.

"Do you think I should get a nose job?" Ruhat asked, changing the subject.

"No," Imani shook her head, "God made you this way and you need to accept it."

"You don't need one," Maysa insisted. "There's nothing wrong with the way you look."

"Yes, you do," Aamal said. "Chop that thing off. Many people in my family did and they're happier for it. Your nose is way too big, and it's holding you back from being pretty."

"That's what I think, too," Ruhat said.

Maysa drew her lips in a thin line. Ruhat's bump

wasn't too bad, even though students sometimes joked around. Her whole family had that nose, and it made Ruhat look unique. Maysa didn't understand why she would change that and why Aamal's words were so harsh. But her words were always harsh. She couldn't recall a time when Aamal was nice.

Maysa wasn't satisfied with her friends, but they were the only ones she had. Aamal and Imani, who both wore *hijabs* like her, made her feel like she belonged somewhere. As the only Muslims in the school, it could be easy to stand out, but together they were a team of sorts. Years ago, Aamal and Ruhat had older brothers attend, but they had graduated. Now it was just this quartet of Muslims in the school. Ruhat, minus the head covering, was a practicing Muslim. They all knew each other's families, celebrated Muslim holidays together, and saw each other at the mosque. Maysa was automatically part of this group because of who and what she was.

Despite all the talking they did, the door was almost done. Maysa had created a huge turkey on the bottom half of the door. Aamal had made a border. Ruhat and Imani were still working on the stuffed cornucopia, but their teacher hadn't expected them to finish today. They would complete the door tomorrow. Before the bell rang, Maysa parted with them to go to the restroom. She didn't ask for a pass since the bathroom was right next to class, around a corner.

She walked in and stood in front of the mirror. Her scarf was askew from all the bending up and down she'd done while decorating. She'd also banged her head against a cabinet in Ms. Montes's room when she had collected the material for the door.

She would never uncover herself in public,

27

particularly around boys. Since she was in the safety of a girls' restroom, and by herself, she took off her scarf and the lace cap underneath so she could tie it again. Her long, wavy hair had become loose in the bun, so she had to redo that, too. Her hair might peek out of the edges of the scarf, so she needed the bun, and the cap was so that the silky scarf wouldn't slip off.

Her hair flowed across her back and shoulders. She ran her fingers through it. When she was little, before she wore *hijab*, she received numerous compliments on it. Then her parents lectured her on modesty and how they expected her to keep her head covered like her mother did, how all the women in their family did, except for some cousins in other parts of the country who wore their hair loose. Maysa wondered what it would be like to stop wearing it outside, but her headscarf had become part of who she was. She couldn't not wear it.

She stretched her elastic hair tie, ready to secure her hair into a bun, but then the elastic broke.

"No!" She opened her book bag, riffling through it to find another elastic band. Because of her haste, she spilled its contents. She groaned in frustration as books, folders, and loose papers fell onto the dirty tiles of the bathroom.

Who knew who might walk in—her classmates had only seen her in *hijab*, and they might not recognize her, or they might gossip about what she looked like without it. *Oh, I finally saw Maysa without her scarf. Her hair is really long. Oh, she looks so much better without it.* She didn't want anything like that to spread. People pretty much left her alone, not asking about her *hijab* or hassling her about it, and she wanted it to stay that way. She only had a few minutes before the bell rang to fix her book bag, hair, and scarf. She shoved her things into her bag. Then someone walked in. Maysa inhaled sharply, upset that someone had intruded on her when she was in a nervous rush. She hoped it was one of her friends rather than a stranger. She bent down, her hair tumbling across her book bag, because she didn't want to face the person.

"Let me help you."

"No, no, no," Maysa protested, shielding her face with her hair.

"Maysa," the girl said.

It sounded like Ruhat, but when she looked up she saw she was wrong. It was Haydee. Her eyes were red, as if she had been crying. Maysa felt only slightly relieved—they were both in vulnerable positions.

She didn't argue with Haydee, who set her things straight in her book bag and zipped it up. "Do you have a rubber band or something I can tie my hair with?" Maysa asked.

Haydee found a hair tie in her pants pocket. "Here you go." She sniffled.

Maysa quickly tied her hair in a bun, put on the lace cap, and placed her scarf on top of that. Haydee stared at her the entire time. "You have really pretty hair," Haydee blurted. "You shouldn't cover it."

She didn't know how to respond to that, so she gave Haydee an awkward smile and changed the subject. "Are you okay?"

"Yeah." Haydee nodded. "I got an upsetting … um … text message. It's really nothing. I walked out of class. I don't think the English teacher will do anything. She seems nice and even asked me what was wrong."

"Oh. Is there anything I can help you with?" Maysa's eyebrows knit together in concern.

Haydee shook her head. "No, no, I'll straighten things out."

"Thank you for the hair tie."

"No problem. Thank you for the chemistry notes yesterday."

They faced each other. Haydee's hazel eyes were getting clearer but she still looked sad, with a drooping bottom lip and tear stains on her cheeks. Maysa wanted to do something for her but didn't know what.

"The chemistry lesson yesterday was hard," Maysa said. She had sat with her friends, while Haydee sat to the side by herself. She wanted to include Haydee in their lab projects—which was the right thing to do to make a new student feel welcome—but she knew her friends would balk at that.

"Science is my worst subject," Haydee confided. "The counselor stuck me in AP since I had it in my last school, but the teacher over there was much easier."

"I can help you in chemistry, if you want," Maysa offered.

Haydee's eyes widened and her lips turned up. "That would be great."

"Let's exchange numbers." That popped out of her mouth. How could she take the words back? But what did it matter? Her parents didn't monitor her texts and calls. And so what if her friends didn't like Haydee? They didn't have to be aware of every little thing in her life.

Haydee whipped out her phone and Maysa was shocked by how cracked it was, although it was functional. They exchanged numbers and added them to their contact lists.

"I'll call or text you if I have any homework questions," Haydee said.

"All right." Maysa smiled. "And, um, can you not tell anyone about this? I don't mean about us talking, but the situation I was in." She felt silly asking Haydee to keep quiet about her loose hair, when most of the girls in their school had flowing locks, but she didn't want her friends to know what happened, Aamal in particular.

"Oh, is it about some religious stuff?" Haydee asked. "It's bad that I saw you like that?"

"Yes and no. I mean, other girls can see me without this." She pointed to her head. "But since I started school with it, I feel like my classmates only know me with a scarf on my head."

"Yeah. I mean, I can see how it would be awkward. That would be like me coming to school with my tats lasered off. People wouldn't recognize me."

Haydee laughed and Maysa joined her. Today Haydee wore full-length pants, so the jaguar and vine on her legs weren't visible. Maysa could see the *H SQUAD* in capital letters on her left hand and the skull on the right. The letters were in a Gothic script, the type Maysa saw in history books, while the skull was plain, more of an outline than something thick and black against Haydee's flesh. Maysa usually didn't care to see tattoos, but Haydee's didn't look horrible. Haydee always wore long sleeves, so Maysa wondered if she had any other tattoos she couldn't see.

The door banged open and in walked Aamal. She narrowed her eyes at Haydee before turning to Maysa. "What are you doing taking so long in here? The bell's about to ring and we need to put all the materials away."

"Okay, I'll be right out. Bye, Haydee."

Outside the restroom, Aamal grilled her. "You were in there forever. What were the two of you talking about?"

None of your business was on the tip of Maysa's tongue. "Nothing. Just chemistry homework."

"Well, don't let her copy off you or anything."

31

What a hypocrite. All Aamal did was copy other people's work instead of doing things on her own. What did she care if others did the same? Anyway, Haydee didn't copy anyone's assignments, because she was always working on her own. She was quiet and polite. Maybe Aamal could learn a few things from her.

"I'm warning you, don't get involved with her," Aamal said, stopping in front of Ms. Montes's door. "The girl is poison."

"No, she's not."

"No, she's not," Aamal mocked in a falsetto voice. "Just watch. She's probably on drugs. Who knows what else she does."

Aamal stomped into the room, letting the door close in Maysa's face. Maysa didn't want to go inside. She didn't want to be in the same room with Aamal, so she fumed in silence. Aamal was the unspoken leader of their clique, with Imani and Ruhat blindly following. Maysa did, too, usually agreeing with her on things, but this she couldn't agree on. She took out her phone and looked at her contacts—her Muslim clique was in there, along with some girls she was friendly with from the mosque, and there were numerous family members.

HAYDEE

That was the only name that stuck out. Maysa's heart fluttered. She could've been in the bathroom talking to Haydee for much longer, but Aamal had to ruin the moment. When she was taking pictures of Haydee, she had the urge to keep on snapping. What was this feeling she had? What was it about this girl that was so magnetic and had captured her attention from the moment they'd met?

Chapter Five

November 26, 2014
10:26 p.m.

Haydee plodded to the bus stop, thinking this was it. She couldn't do the job anymore. Some tricks were kinkier than others. The one she had been with tonight was old enough to be her father, tall and thin like a beanpole, and he had obviously taken an enhancer, because he kept going until she was dry, in pain, and couldn't take it any longer. When she had started crying, he'd choked her to shut her up. She had to tell Rafe about the john. This guy wasn't one of her regulars, and she hoped she wouldn't see him again.

Few cars drove by on the well-lit street and she was the only one at the bus shelter. The bus seemed to take forever, but finally it pulled into view and slowed to a stop. She limped up the stairs, then eased into a seat, took out a compact, and inspected the bruises on her neck. Red ovals marred her skin. She caught people staring at her, and she eyed them until they looked away. Other than the bruised left cheek and her freshly marked neck, there was nothing about her that could give her away. A pair of high heels added four inches to her height, and she wore a dress that hit her thighs. She didn't wear too much makeup, even though Rafe urged her to. When she began this job, she wore makeup like a clown with smoky eyes, bright pink cheeks, and slick, red lips. She'd listened to Rafe and believed everything she saw on TV about prostitutes, but then she'd started to rebel a little bit. She refused the heavy makeup. She sometimes lied about having a family function so she could skip a night or two of *the job*. Occasionally she told Rafe straight out that she didn't want to see a particular john. Tonight she would have to do the same. In her bus seat, she shivered thinking about it. Sometimes he let things go—during those rare times when he was agreeable—and other times he took action. He always raised a fist or open palm to the left side of her face, always hitting her on the same spot.

She got off the bus in the darkness. She gripped her purse closer to her body, since she had been mugged here before. Rafe had become mad at that, too, because she'd had money from johns in her old purse, before some meth head with stringy arms and pockmarked skin had snuck up behind her and taken it all away. Tonight she walked past people who leered at her. Old men sat on stoops. Women looked down at her from balconies. Groups of young men whistled. Haydee's face turned to stone. She felt the change: the baby fat in her cheeks solidified, her right eyebrow rose in a cocked position, and her lips froze into a straight dash. Her muscles tensed. She would fight anyone who tried to touch her ... but not quite. She never fought Rafe. He would hit her, and she did nothing.

Faint music played. The smell of weed wafted underneath doorways, and a couple argued, heavy on curse words. Haydee walked to the end of an apartment building. Rafe lived on the first floor. A metal security gate covered his front door, and Haydee stuck her hand between the top bars and knocked. Standing on a ragged welcome mat, she felt the pounding of his feet from the other side. Despite all the unpleasant sounds and smells of the night, she wanted to stay outdoors. When the door squeaked open, she fought the impulse to run off to the next building, where jasmine bloomed and put off a fragrance so strong that it gave her a slight headache—

she could even stare at the moon at the edge of a nearby park. The night wasn't all that bad. It was the people of the night that created problems.

Rafe was a foot taller than her. He wore a tank top to display his broad chest and muscled arms. His light brown hair curled over his forehead and shoulders, while his bottle-green eyes shone in the muddy darkness of the weak outdoor lighting. He wore a pinky ring, thick rope bracelet, and gold chain. His jewelry flashed as he moved.

"You do Fernando good?" he asked.

Fernando was the beanpole john of the night. She nodded. "Yeah."

"He really wanted Darla, but I had her busy somewhere else."

Through an open bedroom door, Haydee could see Darla. She was lying on the bed, smoking a cigarette and watching TV. She wore a bra and panties, with a heavy mask of makeup. There was a time when that was Haydee. Then Rafe fell for his other hoes. He joked about his *harem* and his *stable*. Ever since he started hitting her, Haydee couldn't bring herself to flirt with Rafe or pretend to be interested in him. It was just business between them now.

"Well, get in and close the door so we can discuss things."

Haydee stepped over the threshold, full of hesitation. She closed the door softly but stayed close, not wanting to be away from it in case she needed to bolt. Darla looked her way, then got up, all legs, a concave stomach, and full chest, and slammed the bedroom door.

She was alone with him. The living room was a mess of full ashtrays and pizza boxes. Haydee used to fantasize that she and Rafe would live together. She'd

clean the apartment, and he'd do some honest work—
stop being a pimp and become an auto mechanic or store
owner or maybe even go back to school since he was a
dropout. When she met him a year ago, she was sort of in
love with him. She'd loved the smell of his cologne, his
green eyes, and his defined arms. He was ten years older
than she was but still boyish.

She'd thought they would be a couple, but then
she realized that he slept with his other hoes. They were
all just pussy and dollar signs to him, nothing more. Her
romantic notions had died. She had believed this way of
life was temporary, just a way for her to get by for a little
while. How wrong she'd been. Sometimes it felt like
Rafe had invaded every part of her life. She even kept her
work clothes and makeup here, because she didn't want
to dress like that at her own home. She had her aunt and
cousins to think about, and she didn't want them to guess
what she was doing.

"Where's the money?" Rafe asked. "I hope he
didn't stiff you. He did that to Darla once and I had to set
him right. You know I take care of you all. I wouldn't let
anyone cheat you … or me."

"No, he didn't stiff me," Haydee said, her face
still like stone. She opened the purse and handed him the
roll of bills, which he promptly pocketed. Every two
weeks—as if she were on an official payroll—he gave
her a set amount. The rest he kept for himself. Haydee
knew that he was making money off her, Darla, and
twelve other hoes she ran into when visiting this
apartment. When she did the math in her head, he could
afford better living conditions than this. He did have a
Mercedes and all that jewelry, though. It was a ghetto
mentality of spending money to look good, while
everything else around him was trashy.

"Fernando called me while you were on the way here." Rafe licked his lips. "You showed him a good time, put all your skills to use. He liked the sampling you gave him, so he wants to book you tomorrow."

"Tomorrow is Thanksgiving," Haydee said. She cringed, backing away and crossing her arms across her body. "I gotta eat with my aunt and cousins."

"Oh yeah, I forgot about Thanksgiving," Rafe said. "Thought it was the next day. I need to see the family, too. Then it'll be Friday."

"Umm, about that…" Haydee paused. "I don't want to see him again. He's too rough. Look at my neck."

Rafe bent down to look. He sucked in his cheeks. "Hmmm, that's not too bad."

"Yes, it is."

"This guy's been a good customer, and there ain't no way you're turning him down. No way. If Darla could handle him, then you can, too."

"I ain't Darla."

Rafe's eyes flashed. "I don't think you know who you're talking to, little girl. If I say you'll fuck Fernando, you're gonna fuck him."

Haydee clenched her jaw. She didn't want to do this anymore. She didn't want to see Rafe again. They weren't even in the same neighborhood. She could walk out and never see him again. Bye-bye. She could change her phone number. She could go live with another aunt, although Aunt Dayana was the one who'd opened her arms and home to her. Because she was always busy, Dayana didn't interfere with her life, and the other family members didn't seem to want her.

"Listen," Rafe said, his voice deepening. He tilted her chin up and forced her to look hard into his eyes. "I can have a talk with Fernando, so he can soften up.

Maybe you just weren't clear that he was hurting you."

He was choking me. He cut off my air. He did it twice. She wanted to say all this, scream it at him, but she didn't out of fear.

"Anyway, you wouldn't want me to stop by your house. I remember dropping you off at your aunt Dayana's. I don't think she should know about what you do here at night when she thinks you're out with friends."

Haydee gulped. She didn't want her aunt learning all this. Her family already had too much heartache, and this would just add to it. She was already a burden. Even though Aunt Dayana said she didn't mind, Haydee didn't believe her. She was an extra mouth to feed and someone else's child to look after—and this would make everything worse.

Rafe pulled away from her and straightened his shoulders. He smiled at her, but then that expression died down. He sneered, his whole face changing, the fullness of his rage taking over—he was empty of charm and oozing words of persuasion. This was the real Rafe.

He pulled his hand back. He hit her on his favorite spot, below her left eye. Haydee fell back against the door and crumpled onto the floor.

Chapter Six

November 27, 2014
11:10 a.m.

Maysa had woken for the morning prayer but had gone back to bed. Since she had the day off from school with the Thanksgiving recess, she had stayed up watching TV: one mindless sitcom after the other, followed by movies. She kept her phone nearby, expecting a text from her friends, but it was as if they had forgotten about her.

Our favorite movie is on, Romeo + Juliet, she had texted them.

The only one who had replied last night was Imani, and that was predictable since she reacted to texts right away. **Okay, will watch it!** she had texted back. Ruhat and Aamal remained quiet. Maysa frowned. She wondered if she was being too sensitive. It was possible that Ruhat and Aamal were tired, sleeping, or busy. But like her, they always had their phones at their sides. She replied to Aamal and Ruhat's texts right away, but when she was the sender, they didn't always get back to her.

"I don't need them," Maysa said to herself as she stretched and got out of bed. She started to check her phone out of habit but immediately set it back down and chastised herself. She didn't need her friends, so why was she checking her phone to see if they had texted her? No, she wouldn't look at it this morning. She wouldn't appear desperate. Her heart sank. She thought about other girls at school who laughed loud, wound their arms around their friends, and huddled in corners to tell secrets. She'd never really had that with these girls. Aamal was the boss of their group, and the others, including her, followed. It was better than being alone.

Maysa went into the kitchen, where her mother was washing dishes. Indoors, only with family around, her mother left her hair uncovered. A long, graying braid trailed down her spine. Her father was out, monitoring his business since his gas stations were open on the holidays.

Her stomach growled. She was in the mood for pancakes and hash browns. She prepared a large frying pan to make both. After her mother finished washing, she began scrubbing the counters. Then she opened the cupboards to arrange their contents. Maysa tried to stay out of her way, using the smallest counter by the stove. She made the pancake mixture and poured on one side of the pan, away from the hash browns side.

"Do you know that boy we met the other day?" her mother asked between scrubs. "Faisal's son?"

"Umm, not really." She recalled Faisal, a family friend she saw occasionally. He had four sons, one who was a few years older than she was, while the others were much younger.

"Well, I was talking to his wife and she thinks that when you're older you would be a good match for her eldest son, Omeed."

"You know I don't want matchmaking."

"We are just looking out for you and your future. The boys we know are successful, or are getting there."

This marriage talk always made Maysa nervous. She imagined a life of unhappiness, tethered to a man she didn't love. She could remember far back in elementary school how her parents' friends were talking about how she would be good for so-and-so. The older generations were always thinking of marriage for their little ones. They never considered that their children would grow up to make their own decisions and follow their own hearts. Despite the pressure from her mom, Maysa knew her mom's views weren't everything. She'd encountered many Muslims who had met their spouses on their own, with no matchmaking necessary. Perhaps she would never marry. She had an older cousin who'd never married and everyone felt sorry for her, but she was a successful businesswoman who didn't seem to need anyone or anything—she was always traveling, buying properties, and doing whatever else she liked. It wasn't a bad life.

Her mother dropped a dish and the porcelain broke into shards. It startled Maysa, who was already on edge with the marriage talk. She poured too fast, splattering oil everywhere, including on herself. Her sleeves had been rolled up and she screamed as oil splattered onto her left arm.

"What is it?" Her mother rushed to her.

She rushed to the sink. Her arm burned, and red ovals and dots appeared. Maysa grimaced. Her mom went into the refrigerator and pulled out a pitcher of cold water, then poured it down Maysa's arm. It felt good, but once that was gone, her skin burned again. She turned off the faucet since it didn't seem to be doing any good.

"How could you be so clumsy?" her mother said. She tsk-tsked. "You used too much oil. You need to look at what you're doing."

"I know that, Mom." Maysa frowned. Her parents always had a way of berating her while loving her at the same time.

"You should have asked me to make you breakfast."

They did that, too—offering to do things for her, as if everything were dangerous. If it were up to them, she'd live in a bubble so she'd never get hurt … but that was impossible. The world was full of aches and pains.

Compared to others her age, Maysa had it easy. She didn't work. Her father didn't want her behind the counter at any of his gas stations. She had a bank account for her allowance, and all her needs were taken care of. Still, something was missing. She felt like she wasn't really living.

This pain at least made her feel something, since it was rare for her to get hurt.

The smoke alarm went off, the shrill sound making both of them jump. Sanaa, who had been watching cartoons, walked into the kitchen, then started screaming.

"Fire, fire!" Sanaa shrieked.

"There's no fire!" Maysa yelled back.

"Go back to the living room," their mother said to her, waving a hand through the smoke. "Nothing's wrong."

Maysa turned off the stovetop while her mother stood on a chair to reach the smoke alarm. She pressed a button and the piercing sound ended. "Do we have aloe vera gel?" she asked. Her skin was already starting to blister.

Her mother shook her head. She stepped off the chair, then crouched down to soothe Sanaa, whose wet face and hiccups pulled on Maysa's heart. That had been quite a scare for her, because in her young mind she probably had worried that the whole house would burn down. Maysa decided that was the last time she'd cook straight out of bed, when she was still half-asleep. She should've eaten a granola bar.

"I'm going to the drugstore," she said. "I'll be right back." Maysa dressed for the outdoors, which meant a scarf and clothing that covered her wrists and ankles. There was a drugstore around the corner that was open on holidays. She'd get the healing gel, as well as some bandages.

Outdoors, it was sunny, with kids playing in yards. She received a few looks from some boys on bicycles, but she was used to that. Her purse was slung across her body and she took out her phone even though she had told herself not to check it earlier this morning. There were no messages from her friends, but there was a missed call. It was dated 8:32 a.m. No one had ever called her that early.

HAYDEE

Haydee had called her? For what? Her eyebrows rose. Why would the new girl call her that early on a Thursday morning, on a holiday? It must have been an accident. She sometimes called people at strange times because her fingers fumbled or a button was pressed in her purse; before cutting off the phone, she would even hear a voice saying, "Hello, hello, hello?" She stopped in her tracks, wondering if she should call back. Her burning arm made the decision—no, not now. From the side of her hand all the way to the middle of her forearm, her skin was on fire.

Thanksgiving in Miami was warm, but there was a nice breeze that drifted up her sleeve. A cold front would have been lovely against her burn. She even daydreamed of snow on her red, blistered skin, although it never snowed in Miami. She picked up her speed, rushing into the drugstore. She narrowly avoided bumping into an elderly man. A child almost ran into her. People gave her looks, but her mind wasn't on them. There were two things that were of the utmost importance: the raging skin of her arm and the missed phone call. She had texted her friends between nine and midnight, but when Imani was the only one to reply, she put her phone on silent to watch movies, which was why she hadn't heard her phone ring. She was a light sleeper and the ring would've woken her up.

Disappointment flooded her. She could've spoken to Haydee. *Why was Haydee so important to her?* She'd been asking herself that question ever since she'd met the girl—Haydee was new and a stranger, so it made no sense that she occupied Maysa's thoughts so much.

Inside the store, Christmas decorations lined several aisles. Gift sets for nail, bath, and skincare lay in the middle of the cosmetics section. With the Thanksgiving recess, she also had winter break on her mind. It would come soon. Two weeks off. In the past it was two lonely weeks, because other than going to the mosque, she really didn't go out much or even hang out with her Muslim clique.

Maysa pulled herself away from the Christmas items and their soapy, fragrant odors. She didn't have too many people to buy things for, and she didn't need anything for herself except for something to heal her burned skin. In the medication aisle, she gasped. She hadn't expected to see her.

Haydee held a cold pack to her chest, and she looked horrible. She was surprised as well, with her mouth open. Her right eye—the good one—focused on Maysa. Red and purple loose, puffy skin mottled her left eye. Maysa was stunned. She was used to the birthmark—or was it really one?—but not this. This was a serious injury. She had questions on the tip of her tongue but couldn't seem to get the words out.

"Oh, hi," Haydee croaked.

Chapter Seven

November 27, 2014
10:30 a.m.

She had done a stupid thing calling Maysa. She had meant to call Aunt Dayana to ask her for a cold pack, but the *M* names were together—her aunt's name was listed as Mendez, Dayana—and her thumb had hit the wrong contact. There had been a cold pack in the fridge weeks ago, but it was gone. Her cousins must have used it or misplaced it. Her eye was throbbing. After Rafe hit her, he cooled off, so she was able to go to his spare bedroom to change, since she kept her hoe clothes and regular clothes separate. Her movements had been slow; her head was woozy and it took her a while to put her arms through sleeves and her legs into jeans.

When she'd dragged herself home last night, her aunt shook her head and yelled at her about what she was doing with her life. *Maleducada*, she had called her. *Bad-mannered. Not brought up well.* Haydee agreed with her. Her aunt grilled her on what had happened, but Haydee shook her head and lied about a crazy bum coming after her. Her aunt's steely eyes were unbelieving. Then Aunt Dayana gave her a frozen bag of peas for her eye, but it felt lumpy and uncomfortable, with the peas shifting as they thawed. She switched to a plastic bag full of ice, but it leaked all over her face and pajama shirt.

At least Maysa hadn't answered the phone. She wouldn't have known what to say. *Oops, wrong number. Sorry to call you so early in the morning. I'm trying to call my aunt since she's out and I wanted her to get me something. Oh, did you do the chemistry homework? What are you doing for Thanksgiving?* Everything would have come out sounding stupid, because the two weren't friends. How did one justify a random call like that? She wouldn't like someone doing that to her. Maysa must have asked herself what the hell she wanted. She had no business calling her today, especially when it was Thanksgiving. She wondered if Maysa even celebrated the holiday, considering the headscarf, but then she felt foolish and bigoted for thinking such a thing. Maysa was an American, and wearing a headscarf didn't mark someone as a foreigner.

Haydee sighed, shifting in bed and returning her attention to the book that was propped against the wall. She turned fully onto her side, smooshing her face into the half-thawed bag of peas to trap it between her numb cheek and the pillow. She flipped the pages. It was a book on Islam that her cousin Lucy had checked out of the library for her sixth grade social studies report. Haydee looked at pictures of Mecca, men with caps on their heads, then the women with their *hijabs*. They were young and old, makeup free and made up. Some had henna tattoos on their hands—the patterns were beautiful, so much classier than her own tattoos, and they were temporary, which was a plus. The women were beautiful. Each chapter of the book was labeled with a country. She was curious about what part of the world Maysa's family was from, since she couldn't tell by name alone. Would she even get that close to the girl to ask when they were so different?

The old, familiar guilt slammed into her, memories of all the wrongs she'd done, the people she'd hurt, trying to scratch through to the surface. She lifted her face off the bag of peas to touch her tender skin. Deep down, so many things ate at her. She hated being so uncomfortable in her own skin. Instead of diminishing into a faint memory, her past continued to haunt her. Especially her gang initiation from a few years back. She'd learned firsthand that some things were unforgivable, that they couldn't be undone. Haydee swallowed, curling her hands into fists, then forcing herself to take slow, deep breaths when she heard the front door open and close, followed by the thud of feet headed to the kitchen.

Her aunt had returned from running an errand. There was only one store in the neighborhood that was open for last minute shopping, where Aunt Dayana purchased butter and sugar. Haydee stepped out of her room to help her spread ingredients on the countertop. As she did so, Aunt Dayana fussed, brushing hair off Haydee's face, licking her finger to clean off stray eyeliner, and pulling down her shirt when it rode up her back and stomach.

"Aunt Dayanaaa." Haydee pretended to be angry, but she couldn't stop herself from smiling. She liked the attention. She wished she'd had this type of attention from her parents when she was little. Instead they had been getting high, drinking, and disappearing.

Her aunt lightly smacked her hip with a dishtowel to get her out of the way. After placing a pie in the oven and spreading herbs on the turkey, her aunt took a break from the kitchen to watch TV with her children. "Come sit with us!" she bellowed from the couch.

"I'm going out!" Haydee said. "I need a cold pack. Be right back."

No one said anything. Haydee was seventeen, and she was a new addition to the family. She left and came back as she pleased, even though she sometimes felt like someone should stop her. Aunt Dayana loved her, gave her advice, and screamed at the top of her lungs to discipline her, but it was too late for anyone to change her. She was almost an adult, had been on her own for a while, and she had received no upbringing from her mom when she had lived with the woman. Her cousins were nice to her, but they were not her siblings. She was too removed from everyone and everything.

She shoved her feet into a pair of boots and paused at the front door, then pivoted on her heel when she realized she'd forgotten one thing. She went back to her tiny bedroom and put a bookmark in the Islam book. She didn't want to lose her place in case her aunt made her bed or her cousin wanted the book back. She wedged the bookmark between the pages, getting one final look at a girl who bore a striking resemblance to Maysa. Haydee's body tingled, the pain in her eye shortly forgotten. With both the girl in the book and Maysa, she had never before taken someone's beauty into this much consideration. Before, she'd acknowledged that other girls were pretty, but with Maysa there was something more—the girl was exquisite. It wasn't just her looks either, but her character. Haydee admired Maysa's sweetness and intelligence. Her eye throbbed again. She had to tend to it, even though she didn't want to pull away from the picture of the Maysa look-alike.

Chapter Eight

November 27, 2014
11:42 a.m.

"What, what—" The question froze on Maysa's lips.

"I can ask you the same thing." Haydee looked at Maysa's burned hand, where a stripe of red flesh was evident below her sleeve.

"I'm here for some bandages and ointment."

Haydee was at that spot, so she grabbed what Maysa needed and handed it to her. Maysa accepted both items with her good hand. "Let me help you," Haydee offered.

"Thank you," Maysa said. "I might have trouble opening my wallet."

The two girls walked to the cashier. Haydee stopped in her tracks in the food aisle, and so did Maysa, whose stomach still growled since she didn't have a chance to eat the breakfast she had been cooking. Since her mother wasn't wasteful, she'd probably finished cooking it by now.

"Do you want coffee?" Haydee asked. "My treat."

"Umm, you don't have to—" Maysa began.

"Yes, I do. I did call you early in the morning and bothered you, I'm sure."

"No, no, you didn't bother me…" Maysa wanted to ask about the phone call, but now wasn't the right time. They were in line in front of a coffee machine with three other people in front of them. She would ask once they had paid for everything. Haydee stood behind her, so close that Maysa could smell the floral scent of her shampoo and soap. She wore a silk shirt unbuttoned at the top and jean shorts, so that her jaguar and vine tattoos were on display. Maysa tried not to stare, but while she waited for her cup to fill, her gaze darted to Haydee's legs, taking in the intricate details of the vine, the curly tendrils of stems and leaves, and the pink flowers dotted throughout. The jaguar was so realistic, as if it were about to leap off of Haydee's flesh. They were not cheap, as her friends had suggested. Aamal made references to "prison tattoos" and "flea market tats" when gossiping about Haydee, but these designs didn't look crude at all.

Maysa got hot chocolate, while Haydee opted for black coffee with sugar. On the way to the register, Maysa tried to think of something to say, but no conversation starters came to mind. Maysa reached for her purse but fumbled with the zipper with her good hand.

"I got this," Haydee said, opening Maysa's purse and pulling out her wallet.

On any other occasion it would have felt awkward to have a stranger go through her purse, but Maysa nodded as Haydee took out the correct dollar amount. She had a good look at Haydee's face up close; she had clear skin, luscious lashes, and lips the color of flower petals. As Haydee paid and grabbed the bag, Maysa couldn't stop staring. Haydee continued to be helpful, holding Maysa's things until they were outside. There were large planters with wide edges on the outskirts of the parking lot, and Maysa and Haydee dropped down on one of them with their drinks between them. Palm fronds brushed against the back of Maysa's head. She thought about her mom—she would tell her that the line at the store was long if she wondered why her daughter was out too long.

"So why did you call me this morning?" Maysa asked.

Haydee took a deep breath, looking down, then back up into Maysa's eyes. "I was trying to call my aunt, but your name and her name were close together."

"Were you in trouble?"

"Yes. Well, not at the time I called, but earlier. Yeah."

Maysa waited, but Haydee didn't provide an explanation for the black eye. Instead she sipped on her coffee. "It was okay you called, though," Maysa said. "I mean, I don't know how much I can help, but, but—"

She wanted to say so much but didn't know how to put her thoughts into words. It was okay to start a friendship. She didn't have to be in her Muslim clique forever, static with those girls, with Aamal in charge and telling them what to think and feel. She could provide a listening ear and kind words to someone who needed it. She didn't know what Haydee's situation was, but she would want someone to reach out to her if she were to get a black eye. Her attention was once again drawn to the jaguar on Haydee's thigh. The flesh around it was smooth, hairless, and light caramel in hue. She lifted her gaze to the *H SQUAD* and skull tattoos.

"I loved them when I first got them, but now I can't stand them," Haydee said. "My tattoos are ugly."

"No, they're not," Maysa protested.

Haydee broke into laughter, then grimaced. "Ouch, that hurts my eye."

Maysa smiled. "I'm not kidding. Your tattoos aren't ugly." There was nothing ugly about her.

Haydee put her coffee down and reached for Maysa's arm. Without touching the injured spot, she caressed her palm over the top of her hand. "Does it hurt?"

Taken aback by Haydee's ticklish fingers, Maysa

snapped her mouth shut. She pried her lips open. "Yes," she said. "It burns. I can tell it'll blister and itch a lot. The area is already blistered."

"How did it happen?"

"I was cooking and I was startled when my mom dropped something."

"Oh, well, my black eye was from messing with the wrong guy, the wrong life."

"I'm sorry."

"No, I deserved it."

Maysa gasped. "No, you don't. No one deserves to be hit."

Haydee still had her hand on hers. There was still so much to find out, but Maysa wasn't going to get the chance to satisfy her curiosity today. She saw a car pull into the parking lot, and the covered head was one she recognized. It was Aamal, and her eyes met Maysa's—even though Aamal wore sunglasses, she turned her head in a direct manner, and Maysa could sense that her group leader was glaring at her. Aamal slowed down to take a good look at the two of them sitting together. Then she drove away to find a spot.

"I have to go," she said, gathering her bag, purse, and unfinished drink. "My mom is waiting for me." *And I can't be seen with you.*

"I'll see you around school," Haydee said, standing up. "I hope your hand heals fast."

"I hope your black eye heals fast."

"Happy Thanksgiving."

"Yeah, happy Thanksgiving."

Haydee leaned toward her and did what many Latinas did by giving her a kiss on the cheek. It was a common greeting and goodbye, but Maysa didn't expect it. Her cheek felt warm from Haydee's lips, as warm as the burst of feelings she found hard to describe. Was she rude not puckering her lips in return? She usually did the same, but it was relatives and close friends who kissed her cheek, not random classmates.

Maysa walked away from the parking lot instead of going around it where she might have to bump into Aamal. She wanted to stay and talk to Haydee, but that couldn't happen. She didn't want Aamal and her friends to say anything and question this meeting with Haydee, because Aamal would definitely throw it in her face later, with accusations and questions about why she was hanging out with the new girl. She turned to look at Haydee one more time.

Haydee crossed the street. Her shirt rippled in the wind, her hips swayed, and her long, wavy hair flew around her. From this position, she looked like an entirely different person. It was as if she'd stepped out of a movie or music video, as if she were on a beach with the breeze blasting her. It didn't matter if Maysa was looking at her back or front, though. She had meant it when she'd told her that her tattoos weren't grotesque.

Her phone vibrated, pulling her from her thoughts of Haydee. She didn't want to open her purse with her bad hand, so she went home first. The spicy scent of chicken marinating hit her the moment she opened the front door. Her parents didn't like the taste of turkey since they never had it in their home country when they were young. Inside the kitchen, Maysa saw that her mother had finished cooking the breakfast that she'd abandoned. It was still warm, so she'd eat it after she used the aloe and checked her phone.

Maysa closed her bedroom door with the back of her foot, broke the seal of the aloe bottle, and squeezed some onto her palm. She rubbed it along her arm, sighing as the cool green gel went to work soothing and healing the blistered skin on her arm and hand. With her good hand, she plucked her phone out of her purse, grimacing when she spotted a text from Aamal.

Why were you with that girl?

Maysa thought back to last night, when she was texting her friends while she watched movies and how only Imani responded with one text. She would do the same to Aamal, so she deleted the message. Aamal would probably give her hell on Monday, when they were back in school. She needed to tell Aamal off, let her know that everything wasn't her business, that she could talk to people outside of school and that it was no big deal.

I know you're there. Answer!

No, Maysa was tempted to reply, but she didn't type out her thoughts.

Fine, see you Monday

That last text was calm, but Maysa had never known Aamal to be a calm person. She was always angry or on the edge of anger. Was it so wrong to talk to Haydee? Surely, Aamal had seen the black eye. But her friends wouldn't care about that since they had made up their minds about Haydee and probably had no sympathy for her either.

You better not be getting close to that girl

Forget Monday. She had to put an end to this now. It was Thanksgiving recess, a four-day weekend. She wouldn't let Aamal terrorize her like this.

Leave me alone and mind your own business!

Maysa's finger hovered over the *send* button. Could she send something that rude and honest? Aamal was always doing that, texting whatever she liked. Maysa's burned hand and arm throbbed underneath the aloe vera. Her lungs felt like there wasn't enough air in the room, and her heart was bursting with the honesty she held back from everyone. She couldn't stand Aamal and she'd wanted to spend the entire afternoon with Haydee before Aamal had intruded with her presence.

She pressed *send*. Maysa sat waiting for another text, but it didn't come. She threw out the bag and receipt, and her phone was still quiet. She checked her e-mail and social media apps, and there was still nothing from Aamal. She put her breakfast in the microwave for a minute and ate it with a slight smile on her face. How long would this elation last? The day was passing by fast, the way days off normally did. Monday would come in no time. She would be in school and would have to face Aamal and her sharp tongue. Her smile faded.

Chapter Nine

November 29, 2014
12:05 p.m.

The weekend was slipping away from her. She could only put off Rafe for so long. She had eaten Thanksgiving dinner Thursday night at home, where half of her relatives ignored her. With her black eye and her mother in prison, something was very wrong with her, and her family let her know it. Many of them treated her as if whatever she had was contagious. Her aunts and uncles who lived clean worried that she might be a bad influence on her cousins who hit the books rather than the streets. Some relatives treated her like a human being, staring at her eye, worried about her. Haydee had wanted to tell them she was okay and that she could take care of herself, even though that sounded like a lie.

Relatives had come in as if the front door revolved, some staying for a half hour while others were there all night. They went from one home to the next, and many came with swollen bellies from eating a feast at someone else's house. They talked and laughed loudly, although their joy hadn't affected Haydee.

Aunt Dayana flew into another fit after all the guests left. She grilled Haydee about her former gang life. Was she in a gang again? Who had touched her? Haydee stuck to the lie that some street thug had attacked her, deciding that wasn't too far from the truth. She touched the faded marks at her throat and swallowed. She was seeing that same client tonight. Maybe it would be better this time, but she doubted it. She sat in bed with her knees drawn up. Her bedroom was minuscule since it was actually a former walk-in closet. Down the hall, in the real bedrooms, her cousins played video games, crying out whenever they won.

Haydee imagined what life would be like in a quiet place, away from her family and away from Rafe. How would she operate if she were alone, with no one influencing her? Would she be a homebody or out all night? Because of how her life had been so far, she worried that she didn't truly know herself. If she peeled away the layers of her absent parents and all the wrong things she had done, would she find a new person underneath all of that?

She also thought about Maysa. The girl had seemed surprised when Haydee had kissed her cheek, but that was something she did when she cared about someone. It was a simple and sweet gesture, but this time it had been different compared to kissing other people's cheeks... Her lips briefly touching Maysa's soft skin made her wonder what it would be like to do other things with her, not just drinking coffee at a store. She wanted proximity, to be friends with the girl. She imagined going places with her, like to a resort on a beach or just finding a silent nook in their school where they could talk. Immersing herself in Maysa's existence, where things were probably better and cleaner, would be amazing, nothing like her own world. Everywhere Haydee went, there seemed to be a problem. She did like the local park during the daytime, but she could forget about it at night because of the drug dealers and groups of men loitering and looking to bother people. On weekends, she hopped onto the bus to Miami Beach for a morning walk. She knew where to go for some quiet time, but there never seemed to be enough. There was always school to worry about, counselors in her business, her aunt fussing about her, and always Rafe.

When her phone vibrated next to her, she rolled her eyes. It had to be *him*. He texted her all times of the day. *What?* she wanted to text. She couldn't be rude to him, though, because that would mean another beating.

How are you?

It was Maysa. Haydee put her legs down and folded them underneath herself to get comfortable. **I'm okay**, she texted back.

Sorry about the other day. I saw my friend in the parking lot and chickened out.

Haydee frowned, thinking about Maysa's friends. They didn't seem receptive toward her, while Maysa was the opposite, friendly and open. **What's the big deal? You can't make any new friends? Just them?**

Aamal is set in her ways.

There were two other covered girls in that group. There was a dark-skinned, quiet one, Imani, and a light one, Aamal. Aamal was the girl who always appeared angry, the one with flared nostrils. She also frowned all the time, making herself look older than she was. Ruhat was the one who went uncovered, with frizzy hair. Anytime Haydee saw her, she thought about straight ironing the girl's messy frizz, because she had done that plenty of times for other girls before. That would never happen, because Ruhat also gave her dirty looks. Haydee sighed thinking about Maysa's horrible friends. Then she went back to texting.

See you Monday, I think my black eye is a lot better, but I won't go to school if it looks very bad. I don't want anyone asking questions.

I hope you don't miss too much school

Well, we can see each other outside of school

She wondered if that text was too bold. What was her excuse to see Maysa? Were they friends? Were they going to study together? She didn't know how to explain to her that they should just hang out like two regular people—one a former gang member and current prostitute, and another from a traditional Muslim household. Haydee waited for another text. She hoped she hadn't scared Maysa by being too pushy or weird. Why was it that people like Rafe and the gang members were so easy to meet, and it had been simple to fall into their ways, but entering Maysa's life was the most difficult thing there was? She had met other girls, former friends, who asked her to smoke a blunt or to share a bottle of rum, as if it was no big deal, but this was a whole different arena. There was a fortress around Maysa.

Sure, Maysa texted. **Coffee and cocoa was nice the other day.**

Was that *sure* just her being polite? It was still a positive word and Haydee's heart soared. A normal, nice girl was interested in her. She smiled and clasped her hands to her chest. A friendship was forming, maybe something else… She wasn't exactly sure what was going on, with this strong attraction to Maysa, but she simply adored the girl and her presence. She wished she had a picture of Maysa to look at, so that when she wasn't there she could admire her olive skin, large brown eyes, and perfect smile. She had hundreds of pictures in her old, cracked phone. The selfies of herself shit-faced after parties, with her arm wrapped around all the wrong people, should be deleted. Who were those people to her anymore? She had stopped seeing all of them. They only wanted to be around her if she was partying, as high and as lowdown as they were, and she hadn't been to a party in months.

See you Monday … maybe, Maysa texted.

I'll try to come.

☐

Maysa gave her a smiley face. Haydee texted her one, too. She smiled in her walk-in closet room, even though it was bleak with the single bed, tall, faded wood dresser, and dusty floor fan. She needed all the smiles she could get, and Maysa was someone who made her smile.

Chapter Ten

December 1, 2014
7:15 a.m.

During the car ride to school, Maysa fiddled with the bandage on her hand. Underneath her sleeve, more bandages covered her forearm, with gauze keeping them in place. The burn spots were red and she had two quarter-sized blisters. She didn't want to pop them and didn't want to go to the doctor either. Now she was reconsidering that. She could tell her father that no, she'd changed her mind and wanted someone to look at her arm. But then her parents might say something about how she was jeopardizing her perfect attendance streak, since those certificates and honors she received from school were so important to them.

Her father dropped her off, and instead of heading to her friends, Maysa hid. Her friends always sat outside building A, where their first period yearbook class was, but she wasn't ready to face Aamal after that series of rude and blunt weekend texts—Aamal had pushed her and she pushed back, which was a first for their clique. Maysa hung out at building B, where the science classes were. When she went on the browser on her phone, she gasped. The front page on one website reported the most recent news about ISIS and the Middle East. She sat on a bench, reading the horrifying news, while a group of freshmen stared at her. Then she got up and stood on another side of the building. She continued getting stares. A girl looked her up and down and snorted, while boys elbowed each other. "*Terrorista!*" a tall boy yelled.

Maysa recognized him as a star football player but didn't know his name. His friends burst into laughter.

Maysa recalled that *terrorista* was in the lyrics to "The Harlem Shake," a song that was popular a few years ago, but that word had another meaning when he had said it … he meant to say that she was a real terrorist. Several other classmates must also have been on top of the news, and they were taking it out on her. It was like there had been people around waiting for her to be alone, outside her clique, so that they could be racist and nasty toward her. More than ever before she realized that her clique was her bubble, her barrier against the rest of the world.

And so she went to another side of the building, the third one. She only had one side left if this one didn't work out. People seemed to mind their business on this side. Maysa sat by herself and pretended to organize a folder, but her hands were sweaty and she dropped a book. A boy picked it up for her, but she didn't even look at him. "Thanks," she muttered. She was outside her element being by herself like this. Ever since freshman year, she had stuck with Aamal, Imani, and Ruhat. She had known them since the beginning of middle school when they started sixth grade together. A year later, in seventh grade, they started to wear the *hijab* … all of them except Ruhat. Their mothers wore them, and since they were in the middle of puberty, it was their time to embrace it as well.

Because Aamal was aggressive, not just with friends but with everyone, she challenged anyone to say something to her. She had a way about her, so that no jock or popular girl wanted to deal with her. When there was a freshman boy who started calling her "towel head" on the first day of high school, all she did was cock her head, glare at him, then curse at him with some of the foulest words Maysa had ever heard. Despite the holy wear, Aamal could swear like a sailor when she was provoked. She did the same with every other boy or girl who hassled them, so everyone left their clique alone. Aamal was their protection. That's why she was the core of their group.

With that good quality, there was also the bad. Aamal didn't want anyone else in their group, and she looked down on people like Haydee and other girls who had tried to befriend one or more of them. During their sophomore year, some girls wanted to get close to them, but Aamal felt like they were nosy and only pretending to be nice. *They think we're exotic*, Aamal would say. *They want to collect friends from all over the world, even though we were born here. They're not really interested in us. They're not like us. They probably think we're good at math, like Asians are, and just want to copy off us. Did you notice that girl hanging all over you and asking about whether or not you finished your homework? I wouldn't trust her. Oh, she asked to come over to try some Pakistani food? That's what restaurants are for.* Aamal had a bunch of silly, even paranoid, reasons why anyone outside their clique wanted to befriend them. It never occurred to her that all types of people could get along and were good for each other. Maysa felt the pull toward Haydee, but Aamal was determined on drawing her away.

Maysa wanted to reach out to someone, so she texted Haydee. **Are you in school?**

No. My eye still doesn't look good

If Haydee were with her, she would feel so much safer. She wrapped her arms around her waist. She was truly alone, unless Aamal forgot her snippy texting tone. How could she, though? She wondered if standing up to Aamal had been the right thing to do. It felt right at the time, but now she worried about her status with her friends. She could have been polite or just ignored her as she had planned on doing, but Aamal had kept pushing, telling her what to do and forbidding her from hanging out with Haydee.

What was Haydee to her? They had only talked a little bit and had hot drinks together. In comparison, she had known Aamal and the clique for years. Maysa felt like she was walking the line between two very different lives, one in which she associated with *others*, and another where she stayed with *them*. She was on the edge, ready to fall either way. She so badly wanted to fall on the Haydee side, to explore a friendship with her, but fear kept her in balance.

When the first bell rang, Maysa continued to dawdle. Instead of going straight to first period, she drank water at a fountain and looked at the newest pieces of art outside the electives wing. The time between bells was getting smaller, yet she continued to move like a turtle.

She entered yearbook class and her eyes met *them*. Her heart jumped at the sight of the clique. Ruhat, Imani, and Aamal stopped talking and followed her movements. The teacher was at her computer while students milled around. They sat at a desk in the middle of the room, went straight to a computer, or gravitated to the teacher's desk to ask Ms. Montes how her holiday weekend was. Maysa had computer work to do on the yearbook software, so she went to one of the ten computers. In order to reach the computer area, she had to walk toward Aamal.

Her breath evened, but she felt *their* eyes on her. What was she doing? Was there no turning back?

"Maysa, sit here," Imani said. "I have so much to tell you about my Thanksgiving weekend. My brother and I drove to Orlando on Friday. It was so much fun."

"I had a fever the entire four days," Ruhat

complained. "I wanted to text you back and watch the movie with you, but I couldn't."

Maysa felt foolish. That's why Imani and Ruhat hadn't texted her during her movie night. Imani was probably packing or doing some other last minute things before her trip, texting her only that one time, while Ruhat was ill. What was Aamal's excuse, though? She only texted her to pry into her life and tell her what to do. Aamal narrowed her eyes at her and stayed silent. Since Imani and Ruhat were being nice to her, it was obvious she was holding back. However, she wouldn't for too long. Maysa had never known her to bottle anything inside, and the late bell rang, preventing Aamal from opening her mouth. Aamal was a good student, listening to the teacher give them assignments. Her gaze traveled from Ms. Montes to Maysa. Her expression was set, because even when she looked at Ms. Montes, her eyes flashed with anger. Heavy mascara and a thin layer of eyeliner made her brown eyes fiercer.

Ms. Montes gave the clique the assignment of taking pictures of five teachers in action. The group got up and went to the teacher's desk, where she unlocked a drawer containing the cameras. Maysa waited until her friends each got a camera, so she wouldn't bump into any of them, then reached out for one, plucking it gently from the teacher's hand. She was so nervous and shaky that she was afraid she'd drop it, so she grabbed on to the camera bag with both hands.

They left the class. In front of her, Imani mentioned the latest ISIS news. "I got dirty looks this morning," she said.

"I took care of that, didn't I?" Aamal said, shrugging as if it were nothing.

"I can't believe you cursed out the cheerleading

captain when she called you a terrorist." Ruhat studied Aamal's profile with a look of admiration.

"This only happens once in a while," Aamal said with a confident lilt to her voice. "ISIS is in the news one minute and then there's something else, but when they are in the news we're going to get looks and comments. My big mouth takes care of it, though."

"It sure does," Imani agreed.

This somewhat comforted Maysa. She wasn't the only one being harassed, and this was why she had been friends with these girls all these years … Muslim girls sticking together. If she had been with her clique a half hour ago, she wouldn't have been bothered, but because of what transpired over the weekend, she couldn't face them.

Aamal was right. This would blow over. Students would find another issue to occupy their minds and other people to pick on tomorrow, yet this morning had been horrible. Maysa continued to hang back, a foot behind everyone. This felt so odd, because she was *usually* huddled close to them, many times even side by side with Aamal. *Usually, usually, usually…* That word echoed in her mind, because everything about Thanksgiving and the time afterward was unusual.

"Why don't the two of you take the upstairs teachers, while Maysa and I work downstairs?" Aamal suggested, although out of her mouth those words sounded like a command.

Ruhat and Imani walked to the stairwell, and Maysa swallowed a lump in her throat as she stared after them. The hallways were quiet. They were outside Ms. Montes's room and Aamal started walking. Maysa breathed a sigh of relief. The text meant nothing. Friends could be sassy and rude to each other—she saw it all the time. It wasn't like dealing with a parent or other adult, because they lectured and held grudges. People her age snapped at each other, and the next day it was as if nothing had ever happened—everyone was friends again, everything was smoothed over, and life was back to normal. Ruhat and Imani were in line, while Maysa wasn't. Perhaps now that Aamal saw that Maysa had some fire in her, she'd soften up and be a true friend.

When they turned the corner, Aamal stopped in her tracks. Maysa walked slightly ahead, looking to see what wing this was. There was a sign in front of her with ten room numbers listed. "I think the first teacher is here," Maysa said in a slight voice.

"And I think you need to learn about respect," Aamal retorted.

Maysa turned to her. Aamal still had anger simmering behind her brown eyes.

"How dare you be so rude to me," Aamal said, getting in Maysa's face. She continued stalking forward, until Maysa's back was against the wall. "If I voice my opinion or ask you to do something out of common sense, you should listen, not just brush me away. I wouldn't do that to you. I would never tell you to mind your own business if you were looking out for me."

But I've never forced my beliefs on you, Maysa wanted to say. "I'm sorry you feel this way," she said instead. "I wanted to be left alone and I was being honest."

"Honest? Sometimes you need to say and do things to make others happy, but instead you were selfish. You just thought about yourself. You don't think about me and the rest of your friends."

"That's not true!"

"Don't raise your voice to me!"

Maysa hadn't realized that she had done so. There had been minor tiffs in the past, things to gloss over. This one, the issue with Haydee, wasn't a minor bump in their friendship. Maysa could tell it meant a lot to her friend that she drop this idea of friendship with Haydee.

"You're making a big deal out of nothing," Maysa ventured, unwilling to be Aamal's victim. "You saw me talking to someone from school. You say I was being rude to you, which I wasn't, and I'm not rude to others either."

"Yeah, you certainly weren't rude to Haydee, especially if you had time to drink coffee with her."

"We were at the store at the same time, that's all."

"And as soon as you saw me, you didn't even stick around," Aamal seethed with flared nostrils. "You walked away."

Maysa couldn't lie and say that she wasn't sure if that had been Aamal in the parking lot—not many people in Miami wore a *hijab*, and she knew what kind of car Aamal drove.

"I burned myself bad and was there for ointment and bandages," Maysa said, lifting up her arm.

"Oh?" Aamal was skeptical. She grabbed Maysa's arm, hard, her fingers pinching through the fabric and bandages and digging into the blisters.

Maysa yelped, pulling her arm back. One of the blisters popped, with that disgusting ooze underneath the bandage. Aamal's eyes widened, but she didn't apologize. Her lips shifted the slightest bit into a grin after treating Maysa in a rough manner.

"Oh, I see, maybe you were in a bad mood because of your burn," Aamal said. "I suppose I get like that sometimes as well. Maybe. I don't recall being rude, though. Perhaps a bit snippy, but not rude. Don't ever treat me like that again."

Aamal turned and headed toward the first class on their list, which belonged to a social studies teacher. Maysa pulled at her sleeve and looked at the moisture seeping through the gauze. She would have to change it soon. She had brought some gauze and a few bandages with her since all weekend she had been checking the blisters, which were looking better but were still oozing. She was prepared in case this happened, but she'd never expected her friend to aggravate a wound … then be pleased by it.

Chapter Eleven

December 5, 2014
9:42 p.m.

Rafe raised his hand, about to hit her. Haydee tensed, ready for the impact. Why was it that out on the streets she was so bold, throwing her own punches? In her previous schools, if a girl wanted to fight her, Haydee had been all for it, pulling hair and punching the opponent in the gut and face. When she had been in the gang, she'd won plenty of fights.

She was surprised when Rafe put his hand down. He wasn't going to punch her, not today. "I'm not going to mess up your face," he said. "Your eye was ugly the other day, not that I'm going to apologize for that since you like defying me. But when you're fugly like that, you keep the clients away. Stop asking me to drop this guy you don't like. You don't gotta like any of these dudes. You fuck them for money, not friendship. You're with them for what, an hour? It's not a lifetime, babe. I talked to Fernando, asked him to be gentler with you. Your neck looks okay, so he didn't choke you. I take care of you like I said I would."

They were at his place and it was just the two of them, which meant that Darla, his current favorite, was out working. Haydee was back from the creep's place, the one she detested, the one who kept asking for her—Fernando. She didn't know what the guy saw in her. He was one of those sadists who sensed when women didn't like him, so he kept going after the same ones. That had to be it. She had other johns who were more decent, even nice toward her, and she was nice back. But with this guy, Fernando, she barely spoke to him, didn't fake an orgasm, and grunted her displeasure. Despite this, Fernando kept calling Rafe to see her. It was now three times total, and she couldn't take it. He hadn't choked her this time, but he was still aggressive, pounding into her to the point that she felt like screaming. He flipped her, pulled her up, and slammed her down as if she were a mannequin, positioning her to his liking. She was sore all over, and she wouldn't be surprised if she found bruises on her body later on.

Haydee fumed. With reluctance, she opened her purse and handed Rafe money. "I need my share today," she said.

Rafe pulled out a roll of cash from his back pocket, adding to it what Haydee had just given him. Then he counted five bills, one hundred dollars total. Haydee made a face. "I'll give you this now and the rest later," he said.

"But, but—" Haydee protested, a sinking feeling in her stomach. He owed her *a lot* more than that. This was nothing. She had done so much work—filthy, degrading work—for practically nothing.

"I have a debt I gotta pay, but I promise you I'll give you the rest Sunday or Monday."

She didn't believe him. She already hated what she was doing, had chickened out too many times of telling Rafe she wanted to stop hooking and couldn't stand her *clients*. Now this. She needed money for her life after high school so she wouldn't be a burden on her aunt for too long. She wanted to move out, but didn't have parents to take care of her. Graduation was definitely happening, but college wasn't a sure thing. She needed some way to support herself and save money for the future. Now Rafe was pulling that from under her feet. This was the first time he wasn't going to pay her what she deserved. What if this was going to happen all the time? That's how people were. They got used to something and kept doing it. People who were takers kept taking, sucking everyone around them dry. Rafe might end up stiffing her every time.

"Come on, you look like the world is ending," Rafe said. "Have I ever failed you before?"

Yes, Haydee thought. *All the time.*

She was tired of standing in the foyer of his dirty apartment with the bongs, beer cans, and takeout boxes strewn everywhere. There was a knock behind her and she jumped. Rafe's large body brushed against hers as he yanked open the door, handing a delivery man some bills—he could afford that—and grabbing a steaming bag of Chinese food.

"Why don't you stick around?"

"I'm not hungry," Haydee said. Her stomach growled. She hoped he hadn't heard that. She left the room before he could convince her to have a taste of rice or noodles.

She itched to *do* something, but Rafe was too powerful. He was taller and wider than she was, and she was aware that he had at least one gun in his apartment. She couldn't forget all the punches that had landed on her face in the past year. No, she couldn't take him on.

In Rafe's spare bedroom, she changed. She kept her clothes in the top drawer of a dresser. In the other drawers were clothes from other girls. It was as if she had her own locker of sorts. She changed into her school uniform shirt and some skinny jeans.

Instead of taking a bus, she walked. Even though she was no longer wearing the tightest, shortest jean shorts and a white tank top with bra straps peeking through, people stared. She was still attractive in her *regular* clothes. Men whistled and catcalled. Women with sunken, bony faces approached her to ask for money. It was warm and humid, not what December should feel like but this was Miami, where there was no winter. In the morning there had been a slight chill, with the briefest of cold fronts settling on the city this week, but it was gone.

While she walked, she thought about her day. She'd gone to school after being absent several days in a row. She had wanted to talk to Maysa, but her friends had surrounded her. The angry girl, Aamal, looked at her with distaste, her nostrils flared and her eyes dark. Ruhat and Imani looked the other way, as if she were trash to be ignored, like maybe if they pretended she didn't exist, she'd vanish.

But Maysa had looked at her. In chemistry class, Maysa had turned around three times to give her a lingering look. Her eyes were shiny and wide. It wasn't Haydee's imagination that Maysa wanted to talk to her, but her friends held her back. Maysa hadn't texted her all week. It had to be her friends. Haydee hoped they wouldn't discourage Maysa, but she knew how it was. It had happened in the past. She'd get close to someone, and others were in the way. Even when she had been in the gang, girls would advise her not to be around so-and-so, because they were from another school, in a rival gang, had an older brother who was a cop … all sorts of excuses, barriers, and threats. Haydee pursed her lips, wishing she could push Maysa's friends away to get closer to her. She pictured herself kissing Maysa's cheek again, holding her hand, and laughing at silly things. She didn't laugh or smile often, yet Maysa made her heart feel light.

Haydee ended up at a restaurant that looked dirty

on the outside, but she came all the time since the food was good. She sat by herself in a corner, drinking both coffee and soda as she waited for a burger and fries. The money Rafe had given her was at least good for dinner, but not much else. When she was a kid, a hundred dollars had seemed like a lot, but these days it was pocket change. It was good for food and a small shopping spree.

She pulled out her phone, but there were no messages. She'd been in her new school for almost a month, but she hadn't gotten too close to anyone. There was no need for anyone to ask about her past or her many absences, and she didn't ask for anyone's pity. Although there was one person who seemed curious, yet nonjudgmental … Maysa. She also seemed sweet, as if she couldn't possibly hurt anyone. Haydee got that vibe from her. What had her mother told her long ago? Always trust your instincts.

What are you doing tonight? Haydee texted. She held her breath, because there she was again with the random calls and messages.

The waitress brought over her burger and fries. She picked up the burger with one hand and bit into it, with the juice and oils from the meat plopping onto the plate beneath it. Her other hand was on the phone, but she had to remove it, because this burger demanded both hands. As she chewed, her phone lit up.

Watching movies, Maysa replied.

Haydee put the burger down and wiped her hands. **What are you watching?**
Titanic
I love that movie!!!
Me too
What part are you on
Jack is sketching Rose

Romantic
I know

Haydee smiled as she squirted ketchup on her fries. It felt weird to do so, because she rarely smiled, but these normal, teenage texts gushing over a movie made her feel good. What else was her phone for if not to have fun with it? To communicate with Rafe so she could meet up with johns? For her aunt and cousins to ask about her whereabouts? After leaving the gang and the last place she'd crashed at, her phone hadn't been that active. After those months of silence and social emptiness, she was interacting with somebody.

Do you want to go to the movies tomorrow? Haydee ventured. **I haven't been to the movies in the longest**

She waited, picking up the burger again, eating more from nervousness rather than hunger. She stuffed three fries into her mouth, then washed them down with a huge gulp of soda. What if Maysa made an excuse and said no? Why would she want to be seen with Haydee? She probably spent her weekends with her yearbook friends.

I'd love to go. What do you want to see?

Haydee coughed, her soda going down the wrong way. The waitress passed by and put a glass of water on her table. "Thank you," she huffed between coughs.

I'm not picky, she replied. She wasn't. She didn't care if they watched a blockbuster movie or something horrid.

Maysa texted her with the closest movie theater and the earliest time it was open. Haydee planned to be there at noon.

See you there, Maysa texted.
Okay

Haydee paid the waitress and walked out with a spring to her step. She had a bag of hot chips in her hand, which she hadn't finished in the restaurant. She chewed on a few of the long pieces covered in orange powder.

Her favorite restaurant was close to one of the places she despised the most—Fernando's building. She hurried past his second-floor apartment. His blinds were broken and over them was a flimsy, graying curtain. His narrow form glided past the window and into an armchair. Never once did he face her, so she guessed he was watching TV. She had no idea what he liked to watch. When she went there, he demanded she take off her clothes and there was some rough foreplay before he started with his abuse. The TV was never on, but he had the radio stuck on some slow jams station, as if that would turn her on. She'd once heard someone call it *baby making music*, but because of Fernando, she saw it as rough, unwanted-sex music.

With her gaze fixated on his window, she stubbed her toe on a large rock. She fantasized about picking up the rock and hurling it at his window, but she wasn't strong enough for that. The lobby door was usually propped open with a brick, probably by kids who didn't have their own key into the building, and it was easy to get in. She could go up there asking for a second round, faking an interest in him, and boom—she could punch him the same way she used to fight in her gang days. She could find a knife in the kitchen and stick it in his flesh, all the way to the hilt.

She had violent thoughts, but she wasn't in the mood to carry out any violence. Even though she didn't have the nerve to tell Rafe *never again* and to deny Fernando her services, she would muster the bravery to do all of that later. She promised herself this school year, that was it. She had to make a move and do things differently. She was in a new school, lived with a reliable relative, and was even making friends—well, one friend, Maysa.

Her heart lifted thinking about tomorrow and what movie they'd see together. Spending time with someone decent and normal was going to be a change. Her relatives were good people, but many of them wanted nothing to do with her. Maysa saw something in her. Haydee wasn't sure what it was, but she wanted to believe there was purity inside her. She walked away from Fernando's building. Into the night she went, with streetlights washing over her as she stuck to main streets. When people attempted to bother her, she didn't hear them. She focused on Maysa's voice, what she could remember of it from the few times the girl had spoken to her.

Chapter Twelve

December 6, 2014
11:06 a.m.

Maysa sat outside the movie theater. The early crowd was small. Only two movies had started, with a few more starting soon. She hadn't made up her mind on what to watch. There were many animated holiday movies, but she wanted to see something more adult like a romance, thriller, or foreign film. Their large posters were above her. The smell of popcorn hit her nose. Her mouth watered as she thought about what she wanted to eat.

She had told her parents that she was going to the movies with a school friend. They didn't ask her who—they automatically assumed Aamal, Imani, or Ruhat. Her parents thought those were the only friends she had, could ever have. No, she was branching out. Fortunately, they hadn't insisted that Sanaa go with her, because sometimes they tried to push her little sister on her when she went out with friends. She had no intentions of babysitting or doing anything else that might turn off Haydee. Today was about getting to know the girl and enjoying someone's company, someone apart from her clique members. They were out of the picture this weekend, since none of them had asked about her whereabouts or invited her to do anything with them.

A pink-and-turquoise scarf laid snug on top of her head. She wore a pink shirt and jeans and even had on mascara and lip gloss. She wanted to look natural and put together, to make a good impression on Haydee.

She could see her in the distance. Haydee wore a loose burgundy shirt and olive-green pants. Her feet were in sandals. When she walked closer, Maysa could see that her toes were painted red. All her tattoos, except for the ones on her hands, were covered. Maysa wondered if Haydee was covering herself to hide her tattoos or if she wanted to mimic Maysa by wearing modest clothes. No matter what Haydee wore, beauty oozed out of her form.

Maysa stood and Haydee got very close. She thought the girl would hug her, but then Haydee stepped back and smiled. Maysa had wanted a hug from her, even though she didn't give or receive hugs that much.

"Have you looked at the listings?" Haydee asked, turning to the posters. Her long, wavy hair fell down her back, hitting her hips.

The two girls walked together until they stopped at a poster of a foreign film. The critics claimed it was *erotic*, *sensual*, and *thrilling*. A man had his arms wrapped around a woman, with his face in her neck and hair, while her face was tilted up, her eyes closed in ecstasy. "This looks good," Haydee said.

"Hmmm," Maysa said. "I don't know. There are subtitles."

"I don't like reading them either, but I don't mind."

There really was nothing else suitable for them. Haydee did a search on her cracked phone and saw that all the other movies had poor ratings, while the one that caught their eye—*Rendezvous on Butterfly Street*—was the most highly rated.

They purchased their tickets and stopped for popcorn. Since Haydee had bought her hot cocoa the other day, Maysa bought her snacks this time around. They went inside the theater and sat together in the back. Even though the seats were spacious, the two girls shifted their bodies and brushed up against each other, getting comfortable. The two turned to each other and smiled during the trailers. Then the movie started. A married woman took a liking to her new business partner. Numerous sex scenes followed this. A jealous husband stalked the two of them. Then there were more sex scenes. She was hot under her scarf and long-sleeved shirt, and the air-conditioned coolness of the theater didn't help. She glanced at Haydee, who had stopped chewing her popcorn. Maysa brought her soda to her lips and gulped. She left some ice chips in her mouth to cool herself off.

When the credits played, the two stood up. They followed the lighted pathway on the floor, which led them out. Maysa blinked, her eyes adjusting to the bright light of the huge floor-to-ceiling windows of the lobby. There was a larger crowd filling the space with commotion, mainly from children walking past them to see the latest animated movies. Maysa looked at the posters again. Maybe she should have picked something safer, because she continued to feel hot. Her face was flushed.

"What do you want to do now?" Haydee asked.

"I don't know," Maysa said. "I don't want to go home. It's too early for that. Do you want to window shop?"

"Hmmm, I can do that later. I don't have too many gifts to buy."

"Me neither."

"My cousins are all at my aunt's laundry place," Haydee said. "They spend the day there helping her or doing their homework. I've gone there a few Saturdays, but it's boring. Since no one's home, we can go to my place. I don't really cook, but I can make sandwiches."

"Sure, let's go," Maysa agreed. Her heart

quickened as she walked out into the balmy outdoors. December in Miami felt like autumn, with a breeze fluttering her clothes. Since it was noon, the sun was beating down right above her, making her head hotter despite the wind. She felt like throwing a bucket of ice over her warm skin. She hoped that Haydee had her air conditioner cranked all the way up. She was curious to see her place. When was the last time she had been to a non-Muslim household? It had to have been in middle school, when some classmates invited her to birthday parties. Before then, during elementary school, classmates had invited her to their homes all the time. Then those invitations started drying up the closer she got to Aamal and her clan. She felt like time had wound back for her, to a pre-Aamal state, because she was exploring a friendship with the new girl.

"This way," Haydee said when Maysa was about to go the wrong direction. She squeezed Maysa's arm.

"Oh, sorry."

"How is your arm, by the way? Are the burns gone?"

"Yes. There are no more blisters, but I have a few small scars. I'm hoping they'll disappear, but I don't think they will." Maysa looked around, seeing if there were any men around. They were alone on the street, with people behind glass inside restaurants and stores. She lifted her sleeve to show some pink discoloration and skin that was still shiny and healing.

"I hope they don't hurt," Haydee said.

"No, they don't," Maysa assured her.

Haydee's hand traveled from Maysa's upper arm to her hand, where she grasped it softly, leading her down the block to her apartment building. Maysa's hand started to sweat, and she hoped that it wasn't turning off Haydee.

Chapter Thirteen

December 6, 2014
1:33 p.m.

Haydee told herself she was holding on to Maysa's hand to lead her in the right direction, but then she wouldn't let go. It felt natural. Maysa's skin was soft and smooth. Haydee's hand was sweating out of nerves. She hoped Maysa couldn't feel it.

She let go of Maysa's hand to unlock the lobby door. When they were inside, she grabbed Maysa's hand again. She didn't care who saw it. A young couple walked past them with a quick glance across Maysa's headscarf and the two joined hands. Haydee evened her breathing. Maysa squeezed her hand and Haydee squeezed back. The two looked into each other's eyes and away. Haydee could look at her forever, but she didn't want to seem like a creeper. They waited for the slow elevator to come down, and the ride up to her floor was slow as well. Maysa's perfume, which smelled like gardenias, permeated the small space. She closed her eyes and inhaled the amazing smell. Haydee couldn't think straight—what would she and Maysa do in her apartment? She thought about the DVDs she had. They could talk. She'd mentioned making sandwiches. Was there enough food for that? Yes, her aunt had gone grocery shopping last night. Her mind buzzed with thoughts. The elevator chimed when they reached her floor.

"How many cousins do you have?" Maysa asked as she walked down the hallway.

"I'm living with three, and then there's my aunt, who's a widow," Haydee explained. "Her husband died in a car accident years ago. My mom's in prison for stealing. My dad … well, I don't know where he's at."

"Oh."

Maysa's face was neutral. She didn't seem to mind this information. Haydee wondered how much she could tell her. Would she ever reveal that she had been in a gang and that she was a hooker, although she desperately wanted to get out of that? Could she tell Maysa what her biggest regret was?

Haydee's apartment was at the very end of the hallway. She unlocked the door, glad that she and her cousins had cleaned that morning. The place had a lot of knick-knacks and toys everywhere, but it was spotless with clean floors and dust-free furniture. Maysa looked around with large eyes, taking everything in.

"I know there's a lot of clutter," Haydee apologized.

"No, it's great," Maysa said. "I love the paintings and all the family pictures."

Her grandfather had been a painter, so many paintings showing scenes of Puerto Rican streets and beaches hung on the living room walls. There were also family pictures, with only a few of them featuring Haydee. Images of her adorable cousins at various ages were in every corner, even on refrigerator magnets.

"Are you hungry?" Haydee asked.

Maysa shook her head. "Not right now."

"Do you want to see my DVD collection?"

"Sure."

She led Maysa to the tiny bedroom. It looked even smaller now that she was bringing someone else into it. Had anyone else seen it other than family? Haydee realized the answer was *no*. She had lived with her aunt for only a few months and had never brought anyone here until now. In her old place, she'd had plenty of people over. Her mom threw birthday parties for her. Her elementary school friends slept over. Her middle school friends watched movies on the large flat screen in the living room. Then her fellow gangbangers would visit. After her mom was sent to prison, Haydee crashed at a gang member's home, which housed other members. At night she would hear gunshots and screams, which woke her up, and she'd have trouble going back to sleep. Haydee shook her head, clearing her mind of those memories.

Maysa sat on the bed since there was nowhere else to sit. There wasn't even a chair or a desk. Haydee sat next to her. From underneath her bed she pulled out a box that was worn at the edges. The cardboard sides bent at the weight of the DVDs. Maysa crouched down to help her and their heads collided, which made them giggle. The two girls brought the box between them.

"I love Leonardo DiCaprio movies," Maysa said, pulling out *The Great Gatsby*. "The movie is gorgeous and the music's amazing."

"You seem to be really into movies," Haydee observed.

"Oh, I love them so much. They swell me up with emotions and take me somewhere else for two hours. If I'm watching a really good one, I don't want it to end. I really want to know what happens to the characters next. Leonardo's movies are my favorite."

"You have something for blond hair and blue eyes?" Haydee teased.

"No, no. I mean, dark hair and dark eyes are wonderful, too," Maysa said.

Haydee laughed. "I was just kidding. I love his acting, too."

Maysa stared at Haydee's face. Her gaze was directed at her eyes, her cheeks, her mouth, and back up again. Haydee had never been through such an intense inspection before. Men usually looked at her body. A few of them briefly looked into her eyes before becoming grabby. Women looked at her tattoos with disgust or at her long hair with admiration—she received many compliments on her hair.

This was something else. Without even touching her, Maysa was caressing Haydee's face with her eyes. Haydee was about to emit a nervous laugh, but she felt like it would be the wrong reaction. This was something different, something special. Maysa took the box of DVDs and pushed them back, so that nothing separated the two of them. She leaned forward, and their lips touched.

Chapter Fourteen

December 6, 2014
1:42 p.m.

In the back of Maysa's mind, she heard a medley of voices of all the people closest to her—family members and her school clique, with Aamal's flared nostrils in view—but another part of her forced out all those voices and images. She focused on Haydee's beautiful face and soft lips. She dipped her hands into her hair and tugged her in closer.

She pulled back so she could breathe. Haydee's face was red, her lips swollen. "I'm, I'm—" Maysa was about to apologize. She didn't know what had come over her. She had never kissed anyone before. She just did it, without thinking too much about it, because of Haydee's proximity, scent, the look in her eyes…

"No, don't apologize," Haydee said.

She looked at Maysa in a way that was so loving, so tender, that it brought tears to her eyes. No one had ever looked at her in such a way before. It was different from a parent or sibling's love, and definitely not like a friend's love, because she had never felt that.

Haydee's tattooed fingers worked on Maysa's *hijab*. She didn't protest. She sat still as Haydee undid the cloth and the cap underneath. Maysa's long hair was in a bun, and Haydee undid that as well. Her long hair tumbled down.

"You're gorgeous," Haydee whispered. They kissed again, this time with Haydee initiating the lip lock.

Maysa's back hit the box of DVDs, so Haydee stepped off the bed to shove the box underneath it. She also locked the door. "Just in case my aunt comes home early," Haydee explained. "But I doubt it."

What was next? Maysa placed her hands on her knees, rubbing against the fabric in nervousness. Haydee was now taking the lead, which Maysa was grateful for since she didn't know what to do. Haydee began to undress, first taking off her shirt, with her unwavering gaze on Maysa the whole time. Maysa's eyes became saucers, devouring the sight of her. She looked like an angel with wavy hair flowing around her.

Maysa trembled. Haydee—clad only in underwear—put her arms around her. Even through her own clothes, Maysa felt the nakedness of Haydee's flesh, the extra warmth and softness of flesh against fabric. "Lie down," she breathed into her ear. Maysa complied, her form so shaky that it was as if she had the chills. It wasn't cold in this room. With the heat between the two girls, it was actually warm, with dots of sweat forming on Maysa's brow.

"Do you want to do this?" Haydee asked.

Maysa nodded, sure of what was about to happen. It had been in the back of her mind for days but she had denied it, thinking she wanted friendship. She wanted that and more. "Yes."

"Don't say it to please me or because you want to experiment," Haydee said. "I don't want to be played like that. You shouldn't do that to yourself either, regretting something you might do."

"No, I'm not playing and I won't regret this … please."

Haydee yanked up the pink shirt that covered Maysa's torso, and she complied by raising her body so that the shirt could be pulled off her neck. Maysa continued to shiver, but the movements were less noticeable. Wherever Haydee's hand landed became a trail of warmth. Maysa was a virgin, and she believed Haydee could sense that. She was tender and patient, not rushing anything.

She covered Maysa's body with kisses. Maysa stopped trembling altogether and responded to everything Haydee did, and she did her best to reciprocate. Haydee's fingers fluttered over her skin unevenly, as if she didn't know where to put her hands, and she breathed hard. Maysa could tell Haydee was as nervous as she was. Sure she was taking charge, but this seemed new to her, too.

"Have you ever been with a girl before?" Haydee asked.

"No." Maysa shook her head. "I've never been with a boy or with a girl." It felt strange saying this aloud, because she had never talked about sex with anyone. Her mother had the talk with her years ago, and she heard things at school. Sometimes her clique made jokes about sex, but no one ever asked *her* what her feelings were about it or what she had experienced.

"I've never been with a girl before either." Haydee's lips curved. Maysa also smiled, knowing that this was something special, something new they could explore together. Their lips joined again, but then Maysa pulled away.

"What are these marks?" Maysa asked, noticing bruises on Haydee's hips.

"I bumped into some furniture."

"Okay," Maysa said, not believing that. There were various bruises all over her body. Maybe her aunt or someone else was beating her, and Haydee had yet to tell her about who blackened her eye Thanksgiving weekend. She figured Haydee would tell her when she was ready.

Haydee scooted away, then stood up, separating herself a few feet from her, with her hair shimmering down her shoulders and her face still and serious. She stared at Maysa, who raised her eyebrows in alarm.

"What is it?" Maysa asked. "Did I do something wrong?"

"No," Haydee said. "It's just funny that I used to have glasses but haven't had a chance to buy new ones yet. I normally see everything blurry, but I see you perfectly. You're one of the most beautiful girls I've ever seen, and I see you crystal clear from where I'm standing."

Maysa was overcome by an indescribable emotion hearing such loving words. It was like a line out of a movie, but it wasn't from some screenwriter.

"Come back here," she said, beckoning Haydee to lie down on the bed again. The girls clung to each other.

Chapter Fifteen

December 6, 2014
2:53 p.m.

Haydee lay in Maysa's arms, the two of them under the covers, when her phone started vibrating. Rafe.

"Who is that?" Maysa asked in a lazy tone.

"No one," Haydee said. She pressed a button to silence the vibrations. Her eyes were wide open, while Maysa opened and closed hers, half-asleep. There was a lump lodged in Haydee's throat, and she had a hard time swallowing it as her hand flipped her phone so she didn't have to view the screen. This was her other life, her nightlife, intruding into the daytime. She rarely dealt with Rafe during the day. He usually texted rather than called.

She hated this so much, having this dual existence. She wanted to be Maysa's girlfriend, not Rafe's whore. And what did he want? Wasn't it enough that he hadn't handed over her hard-earned money yesterday? Even pimps were supposed to have a code of honor, and Rafe wasn't sticking to one.

U there? he texted. **I got 5 clients for tonight. Really need the money. I owe you.**

It was still unclear why he was in debt. Now he was taking that problem out on his hoes, because he was going to ask them to work extra hard for money. Bile rose in her throat and she reached for a water bottle on her nightstand. His intrusion enraged her during what should be a beautiful moment, with Maysa resting in bed after their lovemaking.

Later, Haydee texted. **Busy now, but okay, I understand**

She didn't understand in the least bit, but she had

to get him off her back. She didn't want Maysa to get suspicious, but the truth would have to come out one day. How was she going to tell Maysa? Maysa looked so beautiful and sweet with the covers to her chin. Her hair was smooth and formed a crescent of blackness around the perfect oval of her face. Maysa was the opposite of all her johns, of all the gang members she'd ever worked with, and of all the thugs she'd called classmates in her last school.

Haydee realized something important. Even though she had done horrible things in the past, someone as amazing as Maysa wanted to be with her. She didn't feel worthy—as if she should have resisted Maysa, never bothered to text her and ask her out to the movies—yet she wanted her so badly. She needed this goodness in her life. How would she keep it?

Rafe texted again and Maysa stirred. Haydee powered off her phone. Maysa had to leave soon. Haydee knew that Maysa had her own double life of being a good Muslim girl in a devout household, and this relationship was forbidden. She had even seen it in the news, with Muslims in their home countries denying homosexuality and mistreating gays and lesbians. But in Haydee's eyes, that paled in comparison to her own double life. She was now Maysa's lover during the day, but during the night her body belonged to others.

This felt wrong, especially since Maysa said she had never been with anyone before. Haydee had never been with a virgin. Her own first time had been when she was thirteen, with an older boy who had immediately forgotten about her. All the other boys after that were brief flings or johns, nobody that meant anything to her. This would be different. She had wanted to give Maysa the gift of tingling skin and bursting sensations, and

Maysa had seemed to love what Haydee had done to her. Haydee now knew what *making love* was like. Everything that had happened to her before was meaningless insertion, automatic thrusting, and fake sighs. This was the real thing … with a girl. In the past she'd admired girls and the way they looked, but never figured herself to be a lesbian. Maysa, her looks, her personality, her very being, and the way Haydee reacted to all this changed how she viewed her sexuality. Having Maysa in her life felt right and downright blissful.

She did her best to stay safe and not get pregnant or get diseases, and a recent blood test let her know she was clean. She couldn't bear it if she passed anything along to Maysa. She would get another blood test soon and break away from Rafe.

"You don't have a boyfriend, do you?" Maysa asked, fluttering her eyes open.

"No, I don't." Johns didn't count as boyfriends.

Maysa smiled, which made her face even more radiant. Haydee needed to keep this girl in her life, no matter what.

Chapter Sixteen

December 10, 2014
7:30 a.m.

It was Wednesday and the last time she had seen Haydee was on Saturday, after watching a movie and after time spent in her bedroom. Had it been an hour or two? Maysa didn't even remember how long their lovemaking lasted. It felt so good that time was nonessential. She recalled that she looked at the time on her phone and thought that her parents might worry, so she got dressed and went home. Haydee had also looked rushed, claiming that she needed to visit her aunt's workplace. There was never enough time with her. Even sitting in class, she kept thinking about Haydee. Her friends droned on, and their words sounded meaningless compared to the feelings ready to burst out of her skin. She needed to be with Haydee.

"I need to copy your math homework," Aamal demanded.

"Okay," Ruhat said willingly.

"And I need you to type my English report for me, since you type so much faster than me," she ordered Imani.

"I do type fast," Imani agreed. "I'll help you this afternoon."

Aamal's mouth continued to run as she asked for things from her friends, although Maysa was only half paying attention to her. Many times Aamal reminded her of background noise—an unpleasant whine or buzz that never ended.

"I think Maysa took ghastly pictures of the sports teams," Aamal said.

"They're kind of bad," Ruhat agreed.

"Well, some of the faces are washed out because of sunlight," Imani said. "Not all of them were taken at a bad angle. We can use most of them."

"If only Maysa paid attention to the work she had to do." Aamal shook her head.

Her *friend* was badmouthing her in yearbook class, but Maysa's mind was far away. Ever since she lost her virginity, she had a deeper awareness of the weight of her body, how heavy her breasts were, how there was a throbbing between her legs when she thought about Haydee, and how her skin felt silky—it begged to be touched again. She used to think that it would be a man, a future boyfriend or husband, who would make her feel this way. She had imagined her favorite movie stars and singers would sweep her off her feet. Those were fantasies, and it used to be fantasies that fulfilled her. Now she had a real-life person awakening her body. Since Sunday morning, there had been texts between them, but Haydee had not come to school.

I have a cold, miss you. Will do my best to come to school tomorrow

That had been her Wednesday morning text. Every time she saw someone who looked like Haydee, her eyes followed that person, because it was as if the ghost of Haydee were haunting her. She wanted to see the tattoos, long hair, and stoic face. Instead she was sitting at the computers with her clique.

"Ugh, you're going to have to take some of these over," Aamal said.

"I think they're usable," Ms. Montes said, creeping up behind them. "Aamal, I appreciate how you have a great eye for photography, but you're being too critical. We can crop out the bad parts. I have a great photo editing program to fix some of the things you mentioned."

Aamal flared her nostrils but didn't talk back to the teacher. Sometimes she said snide things to teachers with a smile on her face, as if being helpful, nice, or curious, but she didn't want to get into trouble. In middle school Aamal had been rude to teachers, which her parents had given her hell for, so she'd learned her lesson. She was only cruel to peers.

Maysa hadn't felt bad about Aamal's words concerning her photography until the teacher stepped in. Ms. Montes's kind words were a huge contrast to Aamal's meanness. It made Aamal's cruelty even more obvious, plus Maysa felt like a victim with someone else speaking up for her. Why didn't she do that herself? She had been daydreaming about Haydee, but she should have been more aware of her surroundings. Her eyes started to tear up.

"Can I go to the restroom?" she asked.

"Of course," Ms. Montes said.

She scurried out without looking at the clique so they wouldn't see her eyes. The tears were brimming over by the time she made it into a bathroom stall. She thought about how much she missed Haydee and wanted to be with her. Then there was Aamal's big mouth and permanently enlarged nostrils looming in her mind. Why didn't she have the courage to walk away from all three of them? She wished she could take Imani with her, though, since she was the *nice one*, and they could make a new clique. She had been harboring all these emotions and having a good cry released them.

Are you feeling better? she texted Haydee. **Do you need me to get makeup work?**

Yes, I'm better, Haydee texted her back within

seconds. **My aunt went to the school to give them a doctor's note and pick up work for me**

It's early but I'm already having a bad day. Wish you were here

I wish I could be there for you, tell me everything later

Miss you

Miss you!

She dried her eyes with one hand, her spirit already lighter. Bending to get some tissue, she dropped her phone. Doing her best not to bump into the dirty toilet behind her, she accidentally kicked her phone outside the stall.

The door to the restroom opened. Then her phone was gone. She bent down trying to spot it, but it wasn't there. Whoever had walked in had it. She banged open the stall door. Aamal was in front of her, with the phone in her hand. Her gaze was on the screen, but Maysa snatched the phone away before she could read the text conversation.

"Ouch, you scratched me." Aamal gasped, retracted her hand, and studied a red slash on the side of her index finger. "I'm bleeding!"

Maysa quickly put the phone to sleep. What if Aamal knew her password? That was impossible, since she always made sure to turn the screen anytime she put in the password. *Then again when someone hangs around people too long, they notice every little thing.* Maysa knew Imani's password and she believed she also knew Ruhat's … at least the first two digits. She would have to change her password. No one could know about her and Haydee. The reality of a lesbian relationship slammed into her—people would call it *haram*, sinful. Many would turn against her. She would disappoint her parents, when they were the type of people who flipped out at any sort of shortcoming of hers, even though she didn't see this as a flaw of any kind.

Aamal put her finger in her mouth for a few seconds. "Who are you texting if you're so desperate for me not to see that message?" she asked. "It had to be someone important. Do you have a new friend? Someone not good enough for our group, I'm sure, or you wouldn't be hiding her, or him, from us. Who are you keeping a secret?"

Maysa brushed past Aamal, causing the girl to be unsteady on her feet. First she'd scratched her, and now she'd shoved her. She wasn't in the mood. This was nothing compared to being embarrassed in yearbook class and having the teacher save her. What she had in her phone and in the intermittent moments she spent with Haydee was so much bigger than anything she'd ever experienced.

"Watch it!" Aamal yelled. "What has gotten into you? Okay, maybe I was somewhat harsh just now, but you know I take yearbook seriously. What, are you going to be a crybaby and want an apology?"

"I want nothing from you!" Maysa said. She couldn't believe the reflection in the mirror. Her nostrils flared the same way Aamal's did. Her eyebrows knit together and her mouth twisted into a snarl.

"Wow, just wow. I can't believe you. Maybe you're on the rag. Is it your time of the month? Did your secret online boyfriend, who's super ugly and talks a lot of bullshit, break up with you?"

That was an inside joke of their clique, because they had known other Muslim girls who had online boyfriends. They had never met them in person but felt elated over e-mails and cried over virtual breakups. She herself had never had one, because chat rooms and social media apps bored her. "I'm not talking to you anymore," Maysa said.

"I have some pads if you want," Aamal said, her voice returning to its usual derisive tone. "I'll let our group know not to mess with you today, since you're all bitchy and menstrual. And obviously you *miss* someone, but you won't tell me who."

"Ugh!" Maysa couldn't take her anymore. She stomped out of the restroom and back into class. Ruhat and Imani widened their eyes when they saw the fierce look on her face. Both of them scooted their chairs away, making room for her at the computer station by giving her a few inches of extra space as she cooled off. They left her alone. When Aamal walked in a few minutes later, she smirked. She also whined to the teacher about needing a bandage for a minuscule cut on her hand, so Ms. Montes wrote a pass for her to go to the clinic inside the main office. Aamal not only cheated on many assignments, but she liked to be out of the classroom as much as possible, always with an excuse to be in the bathroom, main office, or elsewhere. She did as she pleased, but Maysa was tired of that. She felt better standing up to Aamal, but she knew her friend and clique leader would be back to her old self in no time. She went from hot to cold, turning cold at the most unexpected times.

"You know Aamal gets that way," Imani said. "You shouldn't take her seriously. Just ignore her when she acts like that. Or do this. It makes me feel better." Imani made that face again, which she did often—flaring her nostrils and frowning in an exaggerated way to look like Aamal. Seeing that expression on Imani, who was so gentle in comparison, was hilarious. Maysa couldn't help but chuckle. Ruhat and Imani also laughed.

"Yeah, she talks shit all the time," Ruhat said, patting Maysa on the back. "You shouldn't cry about it. Do I cry when she says something about my big nose or frizzy hair? Why would I when I know it's the truth? You need thicker skin."

She would need the skin of a dinosaur. It did seem like this year Aamal had gotten meaner, particularly when Haydee had entered the picture. Haydee barely talked to Maysa during school hours, yet Aamal could sense something was up, that Maysa had undergone a change. She was no longer as quiet or as fearful as before. She did fear some things, though. She remembered how a few days ago she was without her clique before school, and all the bigots had seemed to surround her. She also didn't want anyone butting into her and Haydee's business, judging their disparity … the love life between the tattooed new girl and the *hijabi*.

Maysa frowned and chewed on her bottom lip. How much of the text had Aamal really seen? She had read the last part since she threw the word *miss* into her face. Would she be quiet about what she had read?

Chapter Seventeen

December 15, 2014
9:15 p.m.

Haydee was on her way to Rafe's place with the money she'd earned tonight. She also had a bag of hot chips in her hand, munching on a few pieces as she walked. As one foot went in front of the other, she could only think about *her*. It was Monday and Haydee already wished it were the weekend again. Yesterday had been magical. She'd had another date with Maysa, with movies, then time at her place, inside her bedroom-closet. She immediately wanted more of her when they were apart. At school today, Maysa's friends had huddled around her in the morning, and later Haydee had wanted to sit next to her at lunch and in chemistry class, but that was impossible. In that class, fumes twisted around them as they mixed chemicals, with the clique blocking her view of her girlfriend. Haydee had needed a partner, so she worked with some other loner in the back of the room.

She didn't want this relationship to be a secret. She longed to hold hands with Maysa in public. She wanted to kiss her whenever she wanted, but she couldn't. She imagined that Maysa's family and friends would flip out if that were to happen. She wasn't sure how her aunt would take it, since she was the religious type who went to church most Sundays, but she had never heard her say anything against gay people. Based on what she had seen of the clique and what Maysa had said about her family, Haydee knew that Maysa would take the most heat for their relationship. If Haydee were to come out, she doubted anyone would be surprised or even care that much.

How would she ever tell Maysa about what she did for a living? That gnawed on her conscience. How could she share her body with people as nasty as her johns and someone as pure as Maysa? That didn't match up. Haydee would have to tell her about the prostitution one day. It was too big a thing to keep from someone she cared for. No, she didn't just care about her. She loved Maysa. She'd had a cold a few days ago and went ahead and ordered a blood test through her doctor. She was clean, disease-free.

There was also the other thing to reveal: her past in a gang and the terrible things she had done, the worst being what happened during initiation. The memory gripped Haydee, and she stopped halfway across the bridge, putting an arm on the concrete rail to steady herself. This wasn't the safest place to stop at during the night. There were all sorts of people crossing the bridge on foot and in vehicles, and there were the ones living underneath the bridge. She knew about them because when she was a gang member, she had to hurt one of them.

It had happened a year and a half ago. The gang leader, Flor, had told Haydee that she was ready to be in the gang. She had proven herself already by participating in some petty crimes, but now it was the big initiation. Would Haydee be as rough and tough as she spoke? Could she take on anyone? They went to a bridge and found a woman who was tall and sturdy—a homeless woman, judging from her smell and ragged clothes. The orders for the initiation were simple: Haydee would beat the shit out of any woman who looked at her the wrong way or said something insulting to her. Haydee looked hard at the woman, and in turn the lady called her a bitch.

That's when Haydee's claws came out.

Standing yards away from the scene, Flor yelled and ordered Haydee to fight her, and she did. Haydee punched and kicked, with the gang rooting for her. She felt the homeless woman's punches but kept going, twice as fierce as her opponent. They ended up on the ground. She grabbed the woman by her short, loose ponytail and slammed her face into the ground several times.

Haydee had gotten up in a daze and walked away from the bridge, the victor, yet she had felt so empty inside. Then guilt plagued her—whatever happened to that woman? Was she dead or alive? Had someone seen her and called for an ambulance? Had she been someone's sister? She was someone's daughter, but had she been someone's mother? How could she do something like that to a stranger?

And for nothing since those gang members hadn't been loyal to her. Haydee went to juvie for various crimes and none of them had bothered contacting her once she'd left her last detention center. Sometimes she saw familiar faces on the street, but no one approached her to say hi. She was in a different neighborhood, out of their territory, but they still could've reached out to her. She had looked for trouble, in search of someone to hurt, and that experience filled her with guilt and had altered someone else's life completely, she was sure of it. She had revisited that particular bridge to see if the woman was still there, but the homeless had been run out due to community pressure. Haydee hadn't seen anything in the news about the incident, but crime related to the homeless was rarely reported.

Anytime a john or pimp hurt her, she told herself she deserved it. She wanted to feel what that anonymous homeless woman under the bridge had felt. Now her mind was changing. After Maysa entered her life, she didn't want people abusing her body anymore. Haydee believed herself to be a piece of shit, but that's not how Maysa viewed her with her warm brown eyes and open heart. She didn't want to lose her by doing the wrong things repeatedly.

In the past few months, she'd wanted to leave the business, even if Rafe went into a fit of rage. He did that anyway. Many times she had walked into his apartment to see him roughing up one of his girls. Rafe didn't know where Haydee lived, although it would be easy enough for him to ask about her whereabouts. She had given him a wrong address when she'd moved in with her aunt—he had dropped her off at home one day, but she had asked him to stop at the building right behind hers, so she just had to cross an alleyway—yet he could easily have someone follow her. Haydee worried about her safety, but she had to end things with him tonight.

Across the river, houses sparkled with Christmas lights. Once she went into Rafe's neighborhood, which had more apartment buildings than houses, there were some Christmas lights on balconies, as well as trees shining through living room windows. Haydee had helped her aunt put up the Christmas tree a few days ago, even though she wasn't in a Christmas spirit. She had too many demons inside her to enjoy any holy day.

When she saw the police lights outside of Rafe's building, she ducked behind a tree to hide. There were many questionable people in his building—she had seen crack pipes and other drug paraphernalia anytime one of his neighbors opened their doors and she had a glimpse inside.

Her jaw dropped when she saw two officers leading a handcuffed man to a police car. It was Rafe, his green eyes bright underneath the streetlights and filled with alarm. She wondered what the police were arresting him for this time. He had mentioned a criminal record to her, but she knew of no violations since the two met. Was he being arrested for drug possession or pimping?

His eyes met hers and she pulled back, her face against the bark of the tree. She hoped he hadn't recognized her at this distance. If he did, then he would expect her to bail him out—since she was too young, she would have to get one of the older prostitutes or a family member to do that, and she did know where his brother lived. He always mentioned that they had to look out for each other, so he would expect her to notify someone, but she wasn't willing to free him.

After the police drove off, she stayed behind the tree for a few minutes. Then she dashed out, crossing the street and running to his apartment. She looked for a spare key under the welcome mat … actually, it was inside the mat, where a gash had been made between the material. It was deep in there, so she had to shake it, dirt flying into her face and making her cough. The key fell out with a light *clink*. She knocked twice before using it.

"Darla?" she called out.

The place was silent. Whiffs of rotten food and weed hit her nose. Cockroaches scurried and she walked around and away from them. Haydee checked the bedroom and bathroom. He had been alone.

Her fingers were covered in orange powder from the hot chips she had eaten, so she picked up a napkin—upsetting a roach that was underneath it—and wiped her hands. She threw the napkin and the remaining hot chips in a garbage can, which upset another roach that scurried out of the can. Haydee felt around in her front pocket for the roll of money that she was supposed to give Rafe tonight. She would keep it, since he already owed her. He had been in some sort of trouble since he had not been able to pay her last time. He owed her more money, more than what was in her pocket.

She went into a dresser and found a locked metal box. She shook it, hearing both soft and hard things rattling inside the box. His key ring had to be on him. Unsure of whether police officers or Rafe's hoes would barge in on her any second, she dashed into the kitchen and got a knife. She shoved the tip of the knife between the lock and top. The metal twisted, followed by a *pop* as the box flew open. Whatever the police had been there for, they hadn't done a search.

There was a huge wad of bills in there, along with a bag of weed and a bag of assorted pills. She only took what he owed her, which was a few big bills from the stash. She left the rest in the box. Even when she'd been in the gang, she didn't steal, although the other members had. Also, she didn't want to piss off Rafe. If she just took what he owed her, then he couldn't get too mad. Or could he?

With her hard-earned money in her possession, she was through with Rafe. She was sure he would call someone from the police station to bail him out. She wasn't going to do anything on his behalf. She would leave him hanging. He would have to fend for himself, and she never again wanted anything to do with him. The cell phone store was open late, until ten, so she had some time to change her number tonight. She could even get a new phone, since it was time for an upgrade. Next, she would have to come clean with Maysa.

As she was about to leave, a dark gray object sticking out from underneath a mattress caught her eye. She got on her knees and pulled it out. It was a gun, a 9-

millimeter semiautomatic pistol. It wasn't a large gun, yet it seemed huge in her hand.

She looked at the safety lever. She knew enough about guns to know how they worked. In the gang, she had gone to shooting practice with the girls—one of their brothers had a range, and she would tag along. Her ears would ring and she'd close her eyes whenever she heard a bang. She had used a gun a few times on the range, but it wasn't her thing. Some of the members loved that stuff. They shot with both hands, one hand, with their eyes closed, and anything else they could think of.

One hand opened her purse, while the other shoved the gun inside it. She couldn't believe she was doing this, stealing Rafe's gun. She dug deeper between the mattress and box spring and found a tin box full of cartridges, and she took that, too, glad that she had brought her big purse with her tonight. She wasn't really thinking. Her body was on automatic, but somewhere deep in her mind she believed the gun might come in handy.

Chapter Eighteen

December 19, 2014
11:44 a.m.

Are you at lunch, Maysa texted.
Yes, I'm headed to the concession stand, Haydee replied.
I need to see you
Meet me by P.E.
Maysa had received Haydee's new number a few days ago. She wondered about the phone number change but figured that maybe Haydee's contract ran out or she switched providers. Haydee had even bought a new phone.

Thinking about the change in phones was trivial compared to her feelings. Maysa missed Haydee to the point that her skin itched thinking about her. In class, she found herself scratching her nose. A minute later a thigh or calf would itch, which she scratched through the fabric of her clothes. Then it was her arm. Throughout the lessons, she thought of being with Haydee, because seeing her outside of school one day a week, one Saturday or Sunday, was not enough. The texts were not enough. The only thing that was enough was actually being with her.

Students were excited, talking more than usual. People also walked around with bags of Christmas presents and cards. Maysa had received some cards, mainly from her yearbook class. She appreciated it. In the past people acted as if she didn't have any Christmas spirit, when that wasn't true. Her family had a miniature tree next to the living room window so that their home wasn't the only one without Yuletide cheer in the neighborhood. She hoped to spend more time with Haydee during the holiday season with two weeks off school.

There were just a few more hours left before dismissal. She looked forward to winter break, but then afterward it would be back to the same weekend meetings with Haydee that seemed all too brief. How long could she keep that up? In two weekends in a row her parents hadn't asked her about why she was so interested in going to the movies, but if she did that every weekend, they might be suspicious.

When she spotted Haydee in the breezeway joining buildings, she was shocked. Her lips were downturned. She didn't look happy, and Maysa worried that she had said or done something to upset her.

"Are you hungry?" Haydee asked. "Are you going to eat something?"

"I can eat a quick snack later," Maysa replied. "What's going on?"

"I need to tell you something," Haydee said.

"Okay. What is it?"

"Not here." Haydee looked over both her shoulders.

"Where do you want to go?" Maysa asked. She also scanned the area, her head swiveling in every direction, wondering why her girlfriend was acting secretive and vigilant.

"Do you know somewhere private?" Haydee asked.

Maysa did know one place, even though they shouldn't be going there. Ms. Montes's room. She had lunch at this time, too, which meant the room would be empty. The door might be locked, but she knew of a way to get in.

"Follow me," Maysa said, leading the way upstairs. Ms. Montes's room was locked, but the room next to it was unlocked. It was an undecorated classroom with dirty dry erase boards. This was a place where itinerant teachers who weren't assigned a particular classroom taught, whereas Ms. Montes taught in her classroom all day long. In the back of the room was a doorway that led to a room with book carts, shelves, and a coffee maker. This closet space led to five other classroom doors. Through glass windows, she could see that three classes were in session, while the other two doors led to darkness. Maysa went into one of these dark rooms and her eyes adjusted. Ms. Montes's computer monitors were on, so that provided some light. She didn't want to turn on the lights in case a teacher or security monitor walked by.

A raggedy sofa sat in a corner, something Ms. Montes had brought from home to make her classroom cozier. Maysa sat down and Haydee also sat, turning into her so that their knees touched. There was a bag of hot chips making the pocket of her sweater expand.

"This sound is annoying." Haydee took the bag out and put it on a desk. She frowned and looked down at her clasped hands. Maysa suspected that it was a lot more than just the bag of chips that aggravated her.

"What do you have to tell me?" Maysa asked. Her heart pounded at the possibilities of a breakup, her girlfriend cheating on her, and all the other things that could go wrong in a relationship.

Haydee's eyes watered and she was silent. Then she spoke, and Maysa couldn't believe what she was hearing.

Chapter Nineteen

December 19, 2014
11:50 a.m.

The words came out of Haydee's mouth in a rush. Her mother was in prison, which Maysa had already known, but the rest of the information was new to her. Haydee had been in a violent gang, filled with regret about the wrongs she had done with the members. Then there was the finale, the most disgusting part of her life, the one she was ready to renounce forever.

"I am … was … a prostitute," Haydee said. "I have a pimp, well used to have one. I'm through with him. I don't do that anymore and have no intention of doing it again. I want to be with you, not with anyone else."

Maysa's face fell. Her chin quivered, but she remained silent. Haydee knew she was causing her girl pain but kept on talking. It was freeing to finally say everything out loud, because she had never openly called herself a prostitute at school or to anyone outside of the circle that included Rafe, his hoes, and the johns he rounded up for her. Saying it aloud to Maysa meant she could really give it up, that it was over. The confession made her feel like a weight had been released off her entire body, but at the same time she feared Maysa's reaction. Haydee was crying and hiccuping, which was liberating. For too long she'd bottled up her emotions. She wore her stoic face to make others think she didn't care about anything and had no feelings. She did all of that to protect herself, but she was vulnerable inside. She'd had fake friends in the past, her *gang bitches* as she used to call them, but she hadn't opened up like this to them.

Maysa breathed hard, wheezing out of her nose. "I don't know what to say," she said.

"Please tell me you understand." Haydee sniffled. "That I'm no longer these things. I met Rafe, my pimp, and thought it was easy money and would do it for a little while, but I was too scared to leave him. Now I'm leaving. I want to give up all of that because of you."

"How do I know these things are over for you? This is self-destruction and I, I … I just can't be with someone who's a prostitute." Maysa's watery eyes penetrated Haydee's.

Haydee's stomach dropped. What if Maysa ended this relationship? "But I've changed."

"I don't want to share you with anyone. Does that make sense? I want you to be mine and I want to be all yours. I was listening closely. You've been doing this while we were together. I can't have that."

That made all the sense in the world to Haydee. That's how a couple should be, not screwing other people on the side. "Don't say that. You're the one who's inspired me the most to clean up my life. I'm so sorry. I don't want to do that anymore."

"You are no longer these things, right?" Maysa said, grabbing her hand.

"No … never again," Haydee stammered. She looked at Maysa's hand in hers. Could it be that Maysa wanted to continue this relationship? Things weren't over? The warmth of Maysa's love was undeniable, from the look in her eyes to the gentle squeeze of her hand. A mixture of surprise and joy settled over Haydee. "I swear I don't want Rafe or to be in a gang or anything like that."

"Then just be with me."

"That's all I want." Haydee smiled. Relief flooded her. Maysa still wanted her, despite everything she had done wrong in her life.

"Bad things happened to you, and you did things you regretted," Maysa said. "I haven't had the life you had, but I think I might have done similar things if I had been in your shoes. I can't imagine not having responsible parents. I can't imagine living on the streets or staying with gang members, or hearing shots in the dark when I'm trying to sleep. You don't have to live like this, though, because you can have a lot more than that."

"That's why you're too good for me," Haydee said. "I've laid this on you and you're ready to forgive and understand, but I can't even forgive myself."

"That's not true—you are good enough for me and you can forgive yourself. Haydee, just please tell me that this is all behind you. You'll never do any of these things again. It looks like you don't want to. It's all over?"

"It is, I swear. I'm done with Rafe. I haven't seen those gang members in months. I won't even get another tattoo again. I haven't been in a fight in ages. I just walk away when someone messes with me. Ever since Rafe was arrested, I haven't tried to contact him. The only thing I want is to be happy with you."

"I love you," Maysa said, a tear sliding down her face. "That has to be what I'm feeling, and I've never felt it before. If any other person were telling me this, it wouldn't hurt this much."

"I love you, too. I would never do anything to hurt you. I can't stand to see you like this. I've changed and I'll continue to change, you'll see."

Haydee put her forehead against Maysa's, with the headscarf brushing against her skin. She felt empty of tears, empty of every emotion except for love. Maysa's hands went from her waist to her back. The two clutched each other in the darkness, with the monitors going black when the computers went into sleep mode. The only light came from the glass windows of the front and back doors. Haydee caressed Maysa's face, the soft cheeks and the smooth forehead. This was her girl, and Haydee belonged to her.

When Haydee kissed Maysa, she reciprocated, first with soft strokes, then hard ones as tongues explored the insides of mouths. They bit each other's lips and squeezed curves. Maysa's hand traveled underneath Haydee's shirt, settling on the small of her back, while Haydee rubbed Maysa's thighs, her hands sliding up and down the khaki pants. Maysa moaned, and Haydee wanted to keep hearing that. This was risky, doing this inside school, inside a classroom, but they had a few more minutes left for lunch before they had to get back to class.

That's when the front door was flung open and someone walked in. Haydee's eyes widened and she could feel Maysa's body turn rigid. Neither of them had expected to see Aamal.

Chapter Twenty

December 19, 2014
12:00 p.m.

"What is this?" Aamal asked.

The room was still dark, except now that Aamal walked in—through the front door when it had been locked—a slice of rectangular light hit the two girls on the couch. Haydee's shirt rode up her stomach, showing taut abs and a puckered belly button, while Maysa could feel that her scarf was lopsided on top of her head. Both girls had swollen lips.

Aamal had a keychain in her hand, with what looked like Ms. Montes's keys. Maysa recognized the dangling keychains with silhouettes of big cities on them. Whenever Ms. Montes traveled, she bought a keychain. What was Aamal doing with her keys?

"I bumped into Ms. Montes downstairs," Aamal explained. "She's having lunch but asked me to get her flash drive to show something to another teacher. I didn't expect to see you two here."

How could Ms. Montes trust Aamal? Maysa wondered. Aamal somehow charmed her teachers, convincing them to do things, as well as being the willing one to do things for them. She needed her own excuse. "I, um…" Maysa's mouth was dry.

"Maysa thought she dropped a twenty-dollar bill here earlier today," Haydee said, pulling a bill from her back pocket. "It was between these sofa cushions. We flipped these things until we found them."

Haydee certainly thought faster than she did, although she didn't know how believable that lie sounded. Ms. Montes kept nothing valuable around, plus she trusted Maysa. The person who minded was Aamal.

"Whatever," Aamal said, turning on the lights and going to Ms. Montes's drawer. She pulled out a flash drive and was about to walk out, but then she turned to the two of them. "I'll talk to you later, May-saaa."

The name trickled out of Aamal's mouth in the slowest, most threatening manner, with her nose upturned and nostrils flared. Then she left the room. Maysa had to do some damage control.

"Hold on," she told Haydee. "I'll be right back."

She hurried into the hallway and turned a corner into the stairwell, where Aamal seemed to be waiting for her. She faced Maysa, her expression even angrier than it had been a minute ago. "Things are over between us," Aamal said. "My eyes were not deceiving me. I saw what you and that filthy girl were doing. How could you?"

Maysa shook like a leaf, her tongue betraying her. She wanted to say a rebuttal, or at least a lie to cover things up, but her mouth wouldn't open.

"You know, at my elementary school I was called raghead, terrorist, and all sorts of names," Aamal confessed. "I never told you this, but it's true. Those names hurt me so much. I didn't even wear a scarf back then, but classmates saw how my mom dressed whenever she dropped me off at school and those nicknames stuck. It also didn't help that we were poor back then. Having clothes with holes in them and not being able to pay for field trips and other functions also hurt my image."

Maysa's heart softened just a little bit but then hardened again. Imani had told her a few things about how Aamal had a hard life before the clique formed, but this was the first time hearing it straight from Aamal. Still, going through bad things wasn't an excuse for someone to be a perpetual bitch.

"In middle school I decided to change all that, so I befriended you, Imani, and Ruhat," Aamal continued. "It seemed natural, since we're all Muslim girls. I decided to be the strong one. Once someone started on either me or any of you, I opened my big mouth—I know I have one of those, and I use it well. Even though the four of us don't always seem compatible, we stick together for survival. We need to survive in this world, both in school and outside of it. When I was little my father was shot at his corner store, the old one in the bad neighborhood. Did I tell you that?"

"You did," Maysa said. "He was at a cash register and was robbed."

"Of course the robber had to say the most racist things to him. The bullet missed his heart by a few inches. At first I was afraid of everything, thinking that he'd be shot again and that people would say horrible things to me, but then my attitude went the opposite direction and I became strong. I defend myself against anybody, because I don't take anyone's shit. I don't care if someone threatens me, because I'll say what needs to be said."

The crime against Aamal's father had been on the news. Maysa remembered it, even though she had been only seven. Her parents had shaken their heads in fright, worrying about their own business locations and upset by how people assumed they were all terrorists and up to no good.

"You're doing something very foolish, something that can destroy you, our group of friends, and your family," Aamal said. "I don't know if Ruhat and Imani would believe me, though. You've pretended to be so good and quiet for many years. No, they might not believe the truth, but I know what I saw. We've been good friends to you, and this is what you do behind our backs."

Good friends—Maysa felt like huffing when she heard that.

"I don't have to tell them what I saw," Aamal continued. "They do as I say, so I'll just explain we had a falling out and that you don't want to talk to us again."

"Oh, are they your puppets?" Maysa found her voice. "You just snap your fingers and they do what you like?"

"They are decent girls, which is something you don't know about. Your lifestyle doesn't match ours. Watch your tone with me! I can ruin you. I can tell your parents. I can tell everyone."

Maysa's eyes became blurry, because Aamal could do all this. She could open her big mouth and ruin her relationships with Imani and Ruhat and most importantly with her parents. Her parents wouldn't accept a lesbian relationship. The only thing they'd ever had in mind for her was an arranged marriage.

Aamal grinned, looking at Maysa's diffident face. She always knew what to say and when to make someone's insides shatter. They would soon have two weeks off school, which would be a relief since she wouldn't have to see Aamal, but she still could do some damage during and after winter break. Aamal grinned and walked away.

Maysa grabbed the wall, her hands fumbling until she held a rail. Then Haydee was at her side.

"Shhh, don't worry," Haydee soothed.

Maysa's breath steadied, but she didn't want to go anywhere. When the bell rang, she had her next class, which was with her clique. Or were they her clique anymore? She didn't know. Lately it seemed like she didn't care for any of them. Even Imani could seem distant when she was following Aamal's lead. Haydee walked her to math, where she sat by herself in the front and didn't turn back once to look at the clique. In chemistry, she sat next to Haydee, doing a lab with her for the first time.

Since it was the day before winter break, the teacher gave them a simple assignment with a one-page lab sheet rather than the standard two or three sheets. In pairs and trios, students went under a vent hood. They wore gloves and goggles as they poured nitric acid into beakers, then threw various metals into the liquid. A college intern moved between the vent hoods, monitoring the activity, answering questions, and getting equipment. The intern, a young bearded man, handed Maysa some gloves.

Maysa felt squeamish working with the acid, so Haydee did the pouring. Using tongs, Maysa put a penny into the beaker and watched the bubbles. The brown and green layers of the penny transformed, frothing and dissolving. Her eyes were like saucers.

"Cool," the classmates next to her said.

She did not feel like it was cool. Even with her eyes protected by goggles and the plastic hood, she felt vulnerable. The teacher gave them some other metals they could work with. On the board was the structural formula for nitric acid, HNO_3. The teacher's bubbles and lines for the formula chain looked harmless, but in reality, the compound was dangerous. If it could destroy objects like that, Maysa could imagine how it could harm living things.

At the other vent hood was her clique. Imani and Ruhat turned around with questioning eyes. They didn't look angry or disgusted, so Maysa assumed Aamal hadn't said anything yet. That meant she would either slowly torture Maysa, revealing her secret later for the greatest shock value to the people who would look down on her the most, or keep it to herself but be as cruel as possible in other ways. This reminded her of the excommunication practices she read about in history classes.

When people moved away from the vent hood, her clique was directly facing her. The dirty plastic distorted their faces. Aamal grinned, looking straight at Maysa. Her teeth were gray and crooked, her face ashen, and her dark headscarf and black sweater made her look like someone else, something else … a demon or a grim reaper. When Aamal walked away from the hood, her face went back to normal. She directed another sly look at Maysa and packed up her supplies before the bell announced their winter break.

Chapter Twenty-One

December 22, 2014
8:50 a.m.

It was Monday morning. Ever since winter recess had started, Haydee stayed up late and woke up late. Through her sleep, she could hear her cousins and aunt move around as dishes clattered and they spoke to each other, yet they didn't disturb her to the point that she had to get up. All weekend she had slept to the whirring of her dusty fan. There were no more texts from Rafe with her number change.

Her aunt left for work before nine and her cousins joined her. The patter of feet was followed by the slam of the front door. Haydee wanted to enjoy her winter break, so she wasn't going to the coin laundry, although she had a talk with her aunt over the weekend about her workplace. After winter break was over, she was willing to pay Haydee to work at the coin laundry on nights and weekends. It looked like a quiet job, a boring one, punctuated by a few loud kids running around when families went there. Most customers listened to music on earphones, ate snacks from the vending machine, or read a book as they waited for their laundry. The only nuisances were dry cleaning customers who wanted to complain about a mark left on their nice suits and dresses. Haydee was ready for quiet and boring.

She sat up in bed, opened a bag of hot chips, and checked her phone. The sound of crunches filled the room as she ate one chip after another. There were hellos from relatives who were in South Florida for the holidays. Then she saw a good morning text from Maysa. She would text her soon, see when they could go to the mall or watch a movie. She worried about her. That friend, or ex-friend, of hers was a nasty piece of work. Aamal's demeanor and cutting words reminded her of the gang members she used to know. She hoped that Aamal wouldn't create any problems for them. Haydee would do everything in her power to protect Maysa from Aamal and anyone else.

On her phone's browser, she searched Rafe and saw his most recent mugshot, as well as previous ones. His older mugshots reported drug possession, but the newest arrest was for human trafficking and assault. So he was busted for being a pimp and he had attacked someone—either a prostitute or john. Which one of his hoes led to this arrest? Whoever it was, whether it was one or more girls, Rafe got into trouble for abusing them. She wondered if someone bailed him out and if he had been trying to contact her.

Her room was windowless, so Haydee got up, stretched, and ventured into the living room to look out its window. The parking lot was mainly empty, with most people having gone to work. Some neighbors were retired or they worked a night shift. She could hear their footfall above her, as well as some voices in the hallway as people walked to the elevator. Haydee went to her cousins' rooms to look out their windows. No one was lingering behind bushes or on the other side of the street. Maybe Rafe was too busy to care if one of his hoes left him.

She still worried. She had watched police officers arrest him, and he had seen her. Then she took money out of his stash. Haydee's nerves were on edge, even though she hadn't heard from him and no one was outside watching her. A new idea popped into her mind, although she felt uncomfortable acting it out. She was curious, yet didn't want to know the truth.

Back in her room, she opened a drawer, shuffled some underwear out of the way, and looked at the gun. If any of her cousins, the ones who lived with her as well as the ones who visited, touched that thing and got hurt from it, she wouldn't be able to live with herself. She needed a better hiding place for it, so she pulled up her mattress and put the gun under there. Unlike Rafe, she didn't put it on the edge, but deep in the middle.

Then she took out her old phone. It was no longer connected to a network, but it still functioned. She turned it on, the light making the cracks vanish. *NO SERVICE* was in the corner. She went into the settings and turned on the Wi-Fi. There was a blinking box in the living room for everyone in the family to connect their various tablets and laptops. Haydee waited, holding her breath. Then her phone jumped onto the invisible waves emitted from the router.

Her text messages, which were to her old phone number, were still there. She deleted all the ones from Rafe but kept the ones from Maysa. Then she went into a texting app that she used from time to time, holding her breath as it started to update. The number *22* popped up next to the icon.

Haydee gasped. She had used the app a few times to contact Rafe, since he liked it, but she would then return to texting him on his number. Her thumb hovered over the app. She didn't want to read the texts, because they couldn't be any good, but she also had to know if they were really from Rafe and what he wanted from her. She placed her thumb on the icon.

The twenty-two messages began to load. Every single one of them was from him, marked with his profile picture of curly hair and green eyes, and the earliest one was from that morning.

Bitch, I want my money, told ur ass I was gonna pay u back, but u didn't believe me when I was making people pay up money owed to me and paying off a debt

You think just because you changed ur number that I can't find you … I will cuz I own you

Darla bailed me out, but I saw you that night … whore, and you left your nasty orange hot chip prints all over what was left of my money

Haydee's stoic face fell. People had called her every name in the book. Johns had beaten her up, and rival gang members had jumped her, but now she truly felt threatened. She was trying to start a new life, without prostitution, by staying clean and by loving Maysa, and this man wanted to barrel his way through and ruin all of her dreams.

Gonna find you soon and gonna get my money back. U gonna suck dick and fuck when ur told to

Haydee caught her reflection in her dresser mirror. There was no longer a bruise on her left cheek or eye. The *birthmark* that had marked her face for a year was gone. It had become a part of her image, to the point that she ignored it while she was washing her face or putting on makeup, and for it to vanish like that was amazing. It was like looking at a new person. Aunt Dayana said she looked refreshed, while her cousins told her she looked prettier. Without pointing it out, they knew that bruise, that mark of Rafe's, was gone. She didn't want Rafe to hit her ever again, and she certainly didn't want to see Fernando or any of those other disgusting johns who didn't know how to treat a woman, which was why they were paying for a prostitute in the first place.

Rafe wanted his money, but he hadn't mentioned

the gun. He must not have noticed it was missing. He would've mentioned it, because Rafe was the type of person to nickel and dime everything. Even with his weed, he complained if the bag had slightly less than what he asked for from his dealer. He even weighed it, because he didn't want anyone cheating him. He always thought that people owed him like that.

When her old phone beeped, Haydee jumped. It was him, with a new text through the app.

Bitch, I know ur there, because this app lets me know that ur online and reading messages. You'll get what's coming to u

Haydee powered the phone off. The dirty, smudged, cracked screen was dark again. She should never have opened her old phone, because now he knew she had read all his vile messages. It would have been better to pretend she had completely forgotten about him, because some people were like that: super angry, but then they eventually cooled down and let go of things. Now he knew she was up and about, and he would be relentless.

Chapter Twenty-Two

December 22, 2014
12:10 p.m.

They skipped the movies altogether. Instead Maysa had gone straight to Haydee's place. She had been late getting there because of a car accident next to the apartment building. When Maysa had finally arrived, she was all over her girlfriend. They made their way to her tiny bedroom with their arms wrapped around each other's waists.

They lay in bed. Maysa's headscarf was off, as was her sweater. She wore a short-sleeved shirt, which normally felt naked to her. With Haydee she was comfortable in her own skin whether she was naked, partially dressed, or fully dressed. Haydee ran her hands up her arms, squeezing her biceps and shoulders. Maysa closed her eyes in ecstasy but then reopened them with tears.

"What's wrong?" Haydee asked.

"I don't know what's waiting for me when I return to school," Maysa confessed.

"Do you think Aamal will tell everyone about us?"

"I don't know. She's a vindictive, mean person. I could tell people she was seeing things or that she's lying but, but—"

"You're not ashamed of us?" Haydee finished.

"No, I'm not," Maysa said.

"You need to do your best to survive," Haydee advised. "If you feel like you're going to take a lot of shit from friends and family, then you can't let anyone know. But one day, I don't know—what happens after high school? I might want to live with you."

Maysa raised her eyebrows. She had never thought about that before. What was she going to do after high school? Whether or not she was with Haydee or someone else, how would she break this to her family? Maybe she was bisexual, but thinking back on how she viewed the sexes, she had never been into men. If she admired a man, she was just noticing he was handsome. She had never thought about kissing or touching them in any way. She used to think she was in love with Leonardo DiCaprio, but she simply admired his acting and the epic movies he was in—the dramatic music, the close-ups, and suspense that kept her gaze riveted on the screen. Thinking about it some more, she paid more attention to Kate Winslet, Carey Mulligan, and Claire Danes. She was a lesbian. The idea of arranged marriages repulsed her because of the lack of choice—especially if she were forced to marry a man.

The two kissed and cuddled. Their clothes came off. Haydee lit a candle rather than having the harsh light above them ruin the magic of the lazy afternoon. Maysa didn't want the afternoon to end, but Haydee warned her that sometimes her cousins took a break from her aunt's workplace to come home in the middle of the day for a late lunch or early dinner.

Maysa dressed herself with much reluctance. Pulling away from Haydee and getting ready to leave was her least favorite moment of their afternoons spent together. Getting dressed in the morning and walking or taking a bus to see her, followed by her actual presence, were the highlights of any day. Haydee helped Maysa wrap her hair into a bun so she could put the headscarf back on. When she was done with that, Maysa noticed how Haydee pressed a button on her phone to make it light up. It hadn't beeped or chimed all afternoon.

"Are you expecting a call or text?" Maysa asked.

"No."

"Is there a reason why you changed your number?"

"No. I just felt like changing it, starting fresh since I'm at a new school and doing things differently."

Maysa detected a change in Haydee's voice. It became harder, constrained. She was hiding something, but she didn't want to push her. She knew Haydee had been through a lot—maybe someone was harassing her and the number change was necessary. Maysa looked at the make of Haydee's phone. It was a different brand, but the same company. She hadn't changed providers. Even if she had, she still could've kept her old number. Haydee hadn't told her immediately about her past, so maybe later on she'd tell her the real reason behind the number change.

"Will I see you before Christmas?" Maysa asked. "I forgot to bring it today, but I have a gift for you."

"I have one for you, but I need to wrap it," Haydee said.

"So let's see each other tomorrow or the day after. I don't think I can make the excuse of going out every day. When things were good between Aamal and the other girls, I only went out once in a while. My parents might become suspicious. I already told Imani to be my excuse for being out if my parents ever ask. She's the sweetest girl in the bunch and I've done the same for her. I think she went to concerts and other places her parents wouldn't have wanted her to go to, and I told them she was out with me or at my place when she really wasn't. Now that Aamal and I had a falling out, I don't know if Imani is willing to cover for me from now on."

"Baby, I don't want you to get into trouble over me."

"I won't," Maysa said, standing up and kissing her on the forehead.

Maysa straightened her clothes. Haydee opened the door for her and lingered in the hallway until Maysa disappeared inside the elevator. She smiled thinking about how Haydee looked after her. Even though Aamal's big mouth was always in the back of her mind, ready to surface in her thoughts, she'd felt better since winter break started. She didn't have to see the clique and she got to spend more time with Haydee.

On the right side of the building there were hedges between the building and main road. They rustled with the wind. As Maysa walked, she heard footsteps behind her. A woman wearing high heels and too much makeup approached her. Maysa paused, grabbing her purse closer to her body. The stranger walked past her, giving her a penetrating look with deep-set, dark brown eyes. She wore heavy, musky perfume that wrapped around Maysa for a few seconds until she was out of sight.

Maysa took a deep breath. That was nothing, just someone sharing the narrow walkway, probably heading to her car. Vehicles surrounded Maysa once she hit the parking lot. She was taking a shortcut to the bus stop when she saw the stranger get into a car with a green-eyed man who had dirty blond or light brown hair. Maysa couldn't see him clearly since his windshield was dirty. The man got a good look at her, too. She was sure it had to be because of her headscarf. At school, the immature kids made terrorist jokes. Out in public, Maysa received curious stares, not hateful ones.

The man looked angry. Maysa rushed to the bus

stop. Once she sat on the bench, she saw him again a few minutes later. His eyes and the woman's drilled into her. They were by the bus stop, cruising so slowly it was as if time had stopped. When someone honked at them, they sped up. Maysa stared at the black sports car until it turned a corner. Who were they? She pulled out her phone, ready to text Haydee about this, but then she thought she was being silly. The people had not harmed her. They were racist strangers, that's all. She tried to think happier thoughts, so her mind turned to the gift she'd bought Haydee.

It was a set of three silver bracelets. She noticed Haydee sometimes wore bracelets, and silver looked beautiful against her skin. It was a pricey gift, costing more than anything she had ever bought for any of her friends, but she figured that people spent a little more money on their girlfriends. *Girlfriend.* The word reverberated in her mind. She had a girlfriend. She wanted to smile, but she didn't want to do so alone and in public after being spooked just now.

Some people joined her. Maysa continued sitting, but these people were standing, pacing, and shuffling around her with their attention on the road. One elderly woman stepped off the sidewalk and onto the street, using a newspaper to shield her eyes from the sun. When cars came at her, she stepped back on the sidewalk. "It's coming," the elderly woman told them.

Maysa saw that the bus was a few blocks away. Its lighted orange words, with the final destination, were a relief. Sometimes the bus ran slow in this area, but this wait wasn't as bad as previous times. The bus was stuck at a red light. As Maysa anticipated it stopping in front of her, cars were making right turns and driving past her. Then she saw *that* car again.

The man had driven in a circle. Maysa wondered if he was lost, but no, that wasn't it. He came for her, because he slowed down again. Both the green-eyed man and dark-eyed woman gave her dirty looks, this time driving faster with traffic behind them. Maysa inhaled hard. She'd had negative reactions to her *hijab* before, but nothing like this. This wasn't some childish scare tactic, because they had slowed down in front of her twice. Were they planning to hurt her?

The bus *whooshed* as it made its stop. Maysa waited for people to get off, and she eagerly paid and sat down. She went to a window seat on the left side. She put on her earphones, sliding them underneath her scarf, and pretended to listen to music so that no one would talk to her. Her gaze was glued to the outdoors. She wanted to see if the green-eyed driver was following her home.

Are you on the bus? Haydee texted her.

Maysa jumped, not expecting a text.

Yes, she texted back.

Are you okay?

Yes

Why would Haydee check up on her like that? Did she know anything about the couple in the sports car or was this a standard text to see how she was doing? When the bus stopped a few blocks from her house, she got out fast and sprinted home. She turned around to see if the car was there, but it wasn't. She slowed down but continued to be vigilant.

Those people had caught her at the right time, when she had left Haydee's place. They didn't like the way she looked, so they'd tormented her for a few minutes. That's all it was, she convinced herself. Minutes of intimidation. They weren't going to hurt her. They looked older than the people she went to school with, as if they were twenty-something, probably still immature and lacking understanding of people who were different from them. She had no idea who they were, but she had the feeling that Haydee did.

Chapter Twenty-Three

December 22, 2014
1:03 p.m.

Haydee's stomach felt funny and there was a buzzing behind her eyes. She was well rested and well fed. She wasn't on any drugs—she hadn't taken a drag on marijuana in months. Something was wrong, though.

She went to the window and saw Maysa sitting at a bus stop. A black sports car drove past her not once, but twice. Haydee recognized that car. She had seen other cars like it, but this one had a dent in the rear bumper and spinning rims. It was *him*.

All she could think about was Maysa's well-being. She was riveted to the window, with her elbows digging into the sill, watching Maysa's form at the bus stop until it disappeared into a bus. She texted her to see if she was safe. Maysa texted her right back. Yes, she was okay. Haydee held her breath when she saw the car again. Rafe hadn't followed Maysa's bus, but he was still circling her apartment building.

It was daylight, people needed a code to enter the building, and the front door was bolted. Her aunt always told her that if she were alone, to go ahead and use the bolt in addition to the regular lock. Haydee had to get out of here, though. From the way Rafe had circled Maysa, he knew that she was a friend of sorts—she doubted that he knew they were lovers. It dawned on Haydee that Maysa had stuck her head out of the window to look at a car accident that occurred next to the building. The accident was the reason why it had taken Maysa a long time to get there. Haydee had joined her at the open window, getting a good view of the two mangled cars surrounded by ambulance and police lights. Was that when Rafe had seen the two of them together? Had he been scouring her neighborhood and staking her out for several hours? She shivered at that thought. He was serious about getting his money and her body back.

Various relatives were in town and she could stay with them for a while. Ten blocks away were an aunt and uncle who had three guests from New York over for Christmas. Aunt Rosa had been closest to her mother and she had insisted that Haydee stay with them during the winter break, that her house was big enough for all of them, but Haydee didn't want to bother with packing and mingling with the other relatives, some of whom she barely knew. Now she was going to take them up on their offer.

When Aunt Dayana came home later, she would let her know that she was going to stay over with these other relatives. It would be just for a few days, so that Rafe would get off her tail and think that she lived elsewhere. She couldn't let him harm Aunt Dayana and her cousins, or Maysa. He was out for revenge.

Haydee dropped to her knees and dug her hand underneath her mattress to the spot where her money was. It lay inside a dictionary that she had hollowed out with a blade. Within the dictionary was a crudely cut rectangular hole. The ragged edges of the hole scratched her hands as she plucked out the money. She figured no thief would look inside a dictionary, and she had gotten the idea from a movie she had seen. Rafe tended to give her big bills, so she was looking at a small fortune inside this dictionary. She counted the bills in her hands while in her mind she counted how many months she had been prostituting. Ten. She clutched the money tighter, wishing she could give it all back and undo those ten months of STD risks, johns beating her up, and the daily degradation of the job.

Haydee threw the dictionary and a few mystery books she wanted to read inside a duffel bag. She also tossed in an armful of clothes. It would just be for a few days, no more than a week. She would be a good guest at Aunt Rosa's house. She'd cook and clean, go to bed early, and everything else that was normal and good so she wouldn't be an inconvenience or do anything for Aunt Rosa to suggest that she should leave soon. This also meant that she would see less of Maysa. It wasn't as if she'd be able to bring her over to Aunt Rosa's house for a lovemaking session with all those relatives around. She'd have to figure out later how she was going to see her girlfriend. The most important thing was their safety.

After packing her things, she went back to the window. The car circled the block one more time. Then it disappeared. He was gone … for now.

Chapter Twenty-Four

December 22, 2014
7:05 p.m.

Maysa was restless after the incident with the couple following her. She continued to peek out the living room window, but nothing looked out of the ordinary. Her street was quiet, with more cars than usual since neighbors had family over for the holidays. Her parents had given her their password for an online account that streamed movies and TV shows, but she wasn't in the mood to watch anything. Her mind was too frazzled to focus on movies.

She needed to occupy herself with an activity, so she opened her dresser and pulled out a hand mirror, an array of lipsticks, and some tissues. Since she was at home, with no anticipated visitors for the night, her scarf was off for the rest of the day. She sat on her bed and tried on the lipsticks that she had received in gift sets.

Peach was not her color. The beige lipsticks barely registered on her lips. Bunches of tissues with lipstick marks lay next to her leg. She tried the brighter colors. Red looked amazing, especially when she smiled—her teeth looked whiter next to that sharp color. The clique wore mainly eye makeup. She forced those thoughts aside, because it didn't matter what they would think of her if she were to wear lipstick. She was no longer part of their group.

She threw out the tissue and went to the fridge to get a snack. Her father noticed the lipstick right away.

"What is that on your face?" he asked.

"I was trying on lipstick," she replied.

"It looks nice, but don't wear it to school," her

mother said, glancing up from her knitting.

"It does not look good at all," her father countered. "Take it off right away. Did you do your homework?"

"Uhhhh, some of my teachers gave us winter packets—"

"You should start on them right now. I don't want to hear that you didn't do them or you're doing it the night before you return to school. Look at how good Sanaa is being, working so hard tonight."

Maysa frowned at her father's strictness. Her little sister was on her stomach, writing in a notebook, being a good little girl and doing her homework so early during their winter break. He put his feet up and went back to his perusal of magazines. Maysa went to the kitchen for an ice cream bar and headed back to her room. After a few licks, the chocolate blended in with the chemical taste of the lipstick. She threw the lipstick into her purse. She wanted to wear it and see what Haydee thought of the shade.

Her book bag carried the dreaded winter packets her teachers had given her, but she wasn't going to touch them. It was the first Monday of her winter break—what was her father thinking in wanting her to do them right away? Maysa huffed as she plopped her body into a swivel chair, faced her computer, and went online. She typed in the website for streaming movies but then went on another tab to go on her social media sites, which she hadn't visited in weeks. She wanted to know the ugly truth: was Aamal talking about her or not?

On Twitter, Aamal had blocked her, and she told herself she shouldn't care. Since Aamal's Twitter was private, even if she logged out and back in, it wouldn't matter. She wouldn't be able to see her tweets. She only had one hundred followers, but some of them were from their mosque. Maysa finished the ice cream and threw the wrapper into the trashcan underneath the desk. She went on Facebook. Aamal had unfriended her. Ruhat had also unfriended her, which was typical since Ruhat was such a follower. Imani was still her friend, but she also hadn't updated her status in three months. She might have not unfriended her because she wasn't active or had forgotten her password.

Maysa continued to look through these sites, seeing if anyone had posted pictures or gossip about her secret lesbian love life. There was nothing. Maybe Aamal would stop with the unfriending, banish Maysa from their clique and do nothing else. Maysa checked the notices on the very top. People had tagged her in silly memes and pictures, but she ignored them. She went to her messages. Various cousins and friends wished her a great holiday break and sent her early happy New Year messages. Maysa answered them back with her own holiday greetings. Then she clicked on a message that she hadn't expected, dated from Saturday, the day after Aamal had caught her in Ms. Montes's room.

We are ready to forgive you if you accept our conditions.

Her hands were ready to type, but she hesitated. She wasn't sure if she should respond, yet she was curious. She thought the three of them had cut her out of their lives.

What conditions? she typed back.

Maysa returned to the tab with the movies. She scanned the newest titles, wondering if she should watch horror or romance later tonight. While she was deciding, her computer *pinged*. Aamal had sent a message.

Never see Haydee again and you can be our

friend.

No way. She couldn't do that. Maysa clicked on Aamal's profile picture, which was of her in a dark *hijab* with sunglasses and several heavy pendants around her neck. She wore a similar red lipstick shade as the one Maysa had tried on tonight. The picture was from her eldest sister's wedding. Aamal had gone to Italy to attend—for days she had bragged to everyone about how she spent two weeks in Europe, trekking from England to Italy, visiting several countries during her trip. She had made her friends burn with envy, but Maysa had no reason to be jealous of her former friend. Aamal was mean and small-minded. It had taken her too long, up until this school year, to realize that fully.

On Aamal's page were humorous pictures and videos, nothing personal. There were people in her yearbook and honors classes who posted things they later on regretted, that got them into trouble with their friends, parents, and even with the school. The clique was more discreet than they were, saving things for private messages. Still, they could slip up, let others know about her lesbianism. Since Maysa wasn't *out* yet, it would be a rumor, but since there was truth behind it, it would just be a matter of time before everyone knew. She pictured the angry, disappointed looks from her parents.

She spent a few minutes thinking about how she would respond to Aamal—no, she wouldn't. Maysa deleted the message and did some of her own blocking. She blocked Aamal on Facebook. This would give her comfort until she had to see the girl in the hallways and in her classes. That would be something, sitting desks away from someone she blocked online. In real life, it wasn't as easy to block people.

Chapter Twenty-Five

December 29, 2014
7:53 p.m.

The mall was busy. Haydee left the movie theater with Maysa close behind her. Sometimes the two held hands, but then remembered where they were, in front of many people. They moved around with the crowd, and it was hard finding a secluded spot all to themselves. Haydee wanted to kiss Maysa. Her girlfriend looked different tonight—it was the deep red lipstick she wore. She looked like a Muslim supermodel wearing it. She thought about Maysa trailing her lips all over her body, leaving lipstick marks on her skin, but nothing like that would happen tonight. Everywhere they turned, someone was about to bump into them, and they saw faces of classmates interspersed through the crowd. Even though Christmas was over, people were still shopping like crazy.

"This crowd is too much," Haydee said. "I've never seen it this bad."

"Let's go to the top floor," Maysa suggested.

It was on the second floor that they found a bench where they could sit peacefully, with only a few people walking past them. Ever since Haydee had moved in with Aunt Rosa, they were only able to text and see each other out in public. Haydee could have used Aunt Dayana's place during the day, but she didn't want to run into Rafe and his precious Darla.

"I miss you so much," Haydee said. "It's just a few more days, and then I'll be back with Aunt Dayana."

"It seems like forever since I've seen you," Maysa said. "I know it's important for you to stay with family."

"Yeah." Haydee sighed, holding back the truth of the situation.

"I brought my Christmas present … late, I know."

Maysa handed Haydee a small gift bag bursting with red tissue paper, while Haydee pulled from out of her purse a box covered in gold wrapping paper. They both unwrapped their gifts with surprise lighting up their eyes. Haydee put on the silver bracelets, while Maysa spritzed on Chanel perfume.

"I love these bracelets," Haydee gushed.

"This perfume smells amazing," Maysa said, inhaling her wrist.

The two smiled at each other. Haydee was glad that Maysa liked her gift, because she hadn't known what to buy her. Maysa always smelled good, so perfume had seemed like the best present.

"Haydee, I wanted to tell you something, but it seemed too serious to text about," Maysa said. She set the gift box to the side so she could turn her body toward her girlfriend. Their knees touched.

"What is it?" Haydee reached for Maysa's hand.

"The last time I was at your aunt's place, it seemed like this guy was following me—"

"He wasn't. He stayed behind and circled the building. I was watching."

"Who is he?"

Haydee held her breath, wondering how much she should say. She decided to tell the truth. "My former pimp. He's mad because I refuse to work for him, and he thinks I stole from him, which isn't true. Financially, we're both even and we don't owe each other anything."

"Is he violent?"

"Nah. He can be, but I'm not going to worry about him … I don't want to worry about him.

Sometimes I still feel ashamed and dirty, but I tell myself he's in my past. I have nightmares about what life was like with him, but then I have amazing dreams about you. Really, I'll get rid of him someway, somehow. I crashed at my other aunt's place to throw him off so that he'll leave me alone. Once he can't find me for a few days, he's going to chill out. There are plenty of other girls in Miami that he can abuse."

Maysa nodded, and Haydee studied the gentle slopes of her face. She didn't want Maysa to worry about this problem of hers. It had freaked her out when Rafe had targeted Maysa at the bus stop. If he did that again, no matter what, she would have to get between them somehow, whether she had to attack him or call the police. Although, Haydee believed that Rafe wasn't after her girlfriend. He was after her.

The two had pretzels with soda. Then it was getting close to nine. "It's getting late." Maysa yawned. "I don't want to worry my family."

"Okay," Haydee said. "I'll walk you to your bus stop."

That sounded wrong. They were seniors, and they should have cars by now. Maybe Haydee would look into buying her own car since she had all that cash, although it would be hard explaining to her aunt how she'd gotten the money for such a large purchase. Maysa knew how to drive, but her father didn't like it when she borrowed his car. Maysa rolled her eyes whenever she talked about it— he thought she'd crash, that she'd be stupid enough not to put on the headlights at night, or that she would fill her car with friends from school. Her father sounded like a drag.

If Haydee were staying with Aunt Dayana, then the two would be going on the same bus. Aunt Rosa was more out of the way, so she had to go to another stop. Once Maysa was standing at her stop, with three other girls waiting with her, Haydee walked away. She had to turn a corner and walk past a garage. The area around the mall was crowded, but the parking garage areas were desolate.

That's when she heard a voice. "Hey, bitch."

"Huh?" Haydee muttered, turning around, her whole body tense. She didn't see anyone, but she knew that voice. She also recognized the voice that followed.

"I got her!" Darla said.

Someone yanked on Haydee's hair from the back. Then Rafe jumped out of the bushes and onto the sidewalk. "To the garage," Rafe ordered.

Haydee stomped on Darla's high-heeled foot, elbowed her in the stomach, and ran, but Rafe's long legs sped up. Her chin slammed on the pavement. He rolled her over and straddled her. She tried to throw him off but couldn't. She smacked his stomach and ribs, but in her position she couldn't hit too hard. He grabbed both of her wrists in one hand.

Rafe's hot breath sizzled in her ear as he spoke. His curly hair brushed against her face. "You thought I'd never find you," he said. "You moved out of your aunt's place and I don't know where you are right now, but I found you tonight. Darla happened to be shopping here and saw you. She called me because she looks out for me. She knows how to please me. She also knows right from wrong, would never steal from me, and would never leave me like you did."

Despite the blood filling her mouth, Haydee was relieved about one thing—that Rafe didn't know she was staying with Aunt Rosa. Tonight she'd made a bad choice of going to the mall on a busy night. Even though a flurry of people of all ages, speaking various languages, surrounded her, it was possible to bump into someone from her past. It barely felt like the past, because she had only recently left Rafe and that life behind.

Haydee moaned. Her chin and right cheek were sore, but she'd live … if she were able to get him off her.

"What should I do with her?" Rafe asked.

"Slice up her face," Darla said. "It serves her right, plus no one will fuck her. Well, some men might be desperate enough to fuck her, but she won't be pretty no more."

Rafe put his free hand in his back pocket. What was he doing? Haydee thought about whether or not he carried a knife. She remembered seeing knives at his place—not kitchen knives, but pocketknives and a rusty switchblade. She didn't dare scream out loud, because with Rafe's explosive temper there was no telling what he would do next, but she screamed inside her head as she was forced to listen to Darla and Rafe's violent banter.

"We can sell her somewhere, make the money you lost from her," Darla suggested.

"Or I can beat the shit out of her," Rafe said. Haydee struggled but couldn't free her hands from his.

"You can do both."

"Stop!" another voice joined in. "Get off her!"

Chapter Twenty-Six

December 29, 2014
9:00 p.m.

The bus was taking a long time. More people joined Maysa, tapping their feet and sighing. Maysa did the same, her right foot working up and down. She was getting agitated, because she wasn't normally out this late. She texted her mother, apologizing profusely and letting her know that she was safe and almost inside a bus.

I lost track of time
Just get home. It's okay.

Her mom was the more understanding parent. She wouldn't dare text her father, who would tell her how irresponsible she was being out so late. He would also accuse her of taking advantage of her privileges, because they trusted her to be out at night when other Muslim parents had even tighter restrictions around their daughters. She couldn't lose this privilege, so she had to get home as soon as possible.

Maysa turned away from the bus stop crowd so she could peek into her purse to see how much cash she had. She didn't do it often, but sometimes she took a cab around town—usually with others, never by herself. Her father didn't trust her with his car. Her mother had a car, too, but she said it was a clunker and she didn't want it to break down on the road with her teenage daughter having to deal with a tow truck. She had to rely on public transportation but not tonight. The ride to her house wasn't long and she would splurge on a taxi instead.

There was a spot in front of a garage where taxis parked. She walked away and looked back once to make sure the bus hadn't come. No, everyone was still waiting.

That's when she saw a woman in heels standing next to a man on the ground. The man looked enormous. When Maysa got closer to them, she saw that the man was on top of another woman, which was why his form looked huge from a distance. She recognized the long hair and red shirt … it was Haydee who was underneath him.

"Stop!" Maysa screamed. "Get off her!"

"Don't listen to her, Rafe!" the woman ordered. It had to be Darla, Rafe's favorite prostitute, and this was Rafe, the pimp Haydee had told her about.

Rafe jumped off Haydee, but the attention turned to Maysa. As Darla stood watch over Haydee, Rafe advanced toward Maysa, with a knife in his hand. The metal glinted under the streetlight. Maysa's mouth opened into a silent gasp. She had no words for this … a scene from a horror movie, a news piece narrated by a melodramatic anchor, or a page from a grisly novel. This was happening to her, the sheltered girl that she was, that she used to be.

"Oh, you fucking girls now?" Rafe said, his chin tilting toward Haydee.

"Yeah, their hands were all over each other," Darla said. "I saw them. And she's the one who was always at Haydee's apartment."

"You a muff diver? And you got yourself an A-rab girl? Watch out." Rafe then turned his eyes to Maysa. "You know, I know plenty of men who'd love to fuck a raghead, and you're not hard on the eyes."

"Hmmm, I knew some A-rab whore, straight from Egypt, and she made a ton of money," Darla chimed in. "I knew her back when I lived in Atlanta. Men like exotic women, the kind they've never had before."

"There's always room in my stable. Come to poppa."

Maysa couldn't believe they were speaking to her like this. How could this man have been part of Haydee's life? When Rafe walked toward her, she leaped into action. There was an opening into the garage and she ran into it. For a few seconds there was darkness, and then there was bright light as she stepped into an area with rectangles of fluorescent lamps above her. A young couple smiled and laughed as they headed to their car. Maysa registered snatches of their conversation as they spoke about the comedy movie they just saw.

"You have to help me!" Maysa screamed. "There's a man with a knife. Help!"

The couple stopped in their tracks. They wore alarmed, yet detached, expressions, as if they didn't want to get involved. They got into their car.

"Help me!" Maysa screamed again. This time a tall, burly man wearing a security uniform walked over to her. "Out here, out here…"

Maysa led the man to the dark passageway, toward the outdoors. Her eyes burned with tears, because in that minute away from Haydee anything could have happened. Rafe might have knifed her, or the couple could have kidnapped her, and all because she dared to walk away instead of fight back. She knew she had no means of hurting the man Haydee called *Rafe*, but in her pursuit of help she felt like a coward.

Haydee was struggling to sit up, and she was all alone. With a torn sleeve, Haydee swiped at a bloody scrape on her chin. Maysa ran to her, gripped her gently by the arm, and helped her get up.

"Where are they?" Maysa asked.

"I don't know." Haydee shook her head. "They

went to the other garage. After you left and screamed for help, they ran off. I'm hurt from falling, but they didn't do anything else to me."

The two girls and the security guard looked ahead, and Rafe's black sports car screeched out of the garage opposite from theirs. Maysa's jaw dropped when she caught a glimpse of Rafe's profile—his face was becoming familiar now that he was following her—but he didn't stop to say or do anything. It was Darla who stuck her heavily made-up face out of the window. Her hand darted out and she gave all of them the finger before they sped off.

"We need the police to take down a report," the security guard said. "We also need to get your friend checked."

"I'm okay," Haydee insisted. "I don't want to go to any hospital."

Sirens sounded and both girls trembled, edging closer together. When Maysa's sleeve brushed against Haydee's, she reached down and squeezed her hand. "I'm so glad they ran off," Maysa whispered, her voice cracking.

The police soon came by to get a statement from them. Haydee shook her head, and Maysa understood that Haydee didn't want her mentioning Rafe and how he was stalking her. That could get him into jail, but that would also unearth Haydee's past as one of his prostitutes. Maysa told the police about what she saw and told them that she had never seen the man or woman before. Haydee said the same thing. Maysa's adrenaline was going haywire from the situation and all the lying that came afterward. She held her breath, wondering how much longer she could handle this. She pressed the home button of her phone to look at the time, eager to slink away and go home.

"Did they try to snatch your purses?" a female officer asked.

"No," Maysa said.

"Some random, violent attack," the security guard muttered.

"Hate crime," one young officer said under his breath.

Maysa frowned, because she hated how talk always turned to her headscarf and her religion. Just because bad things happened to her didn't automatically make the incidents a hate crime. It wasn't even a hate crime about sexual orientation. Haydee's ex-pimp was furious that she had left him. She had the sense that Haydee left abruptly, cutting him off without an explanation. She wanted to know everything, though. Was this man after not just Haydee, but her, too?

There were no security cameras nearby. Some cameras were inside the garage and around the exits and entrances, but not where the attack happened. There was no use lingering any longer. The officers offered to drive Maysa and Haydee home. Maysa wasn't going to turn that down, since she should've been home already. Her parents were going to be very intrusive on why a police car was dropping her off. She had to think of a way to explain that. She hated worrying about that when she'd almost lost Haydee tonight.

Inside the car, her jaw dropped when she saw the steel mesh cage that protected officers from violent criminals. During the ride, she stared at neon displays in front of stores and recognized most of the street signs. Haydee was doing the same, her gaze bouncing everywhere. Maysa couldn't believe that a short and simple date ended with them in the back of a police car.

She hoped this would be the last time she had to ride in any sort of emergency vehicle.

Chapter Twenty-Seven

January 1, 2014
12:03 a.m.

Are you still in trouble with your parents?
Haydee texted.

Not anymore, Maysa replied. **They seem okay now**

Can we see each other today

I'll let you know. Probably. My parents are visiting friends all day. They'll take my little sister along, so I don't have to babysit, and I can tell them I'm not feeling well.

Uh-oh. Don't jinx yourself. When you say you're sick and you're not then you really become sick

LOL

What are you doing right now

Just finished watching some countdown

Happy New Year

Happy New Year

Haydee itched to hold and kiss Maysa. She had seen in movies that people should ring in a new year with a kiss for good luck.

Ever since that night when Darla and Rafe had attacked her, Maysa's parents had her on lockdown. The police first took Haydee home, before dropping Maysa off at her house. Maysa's parents were furious, wondering why she was involved with the police and why she had been a witness to an assault. Maysa had told them that she saw some random girl being attacked and tried to stop it, revealing the partial truth without telling them she knew the victim. They worried that she could've been a victim, too. Her parents sounded strict, and Maysa assured Haydee that they were.

Since Haydee thought the police almost seizing Rafe put a scare into him, she was back to living with Aunt Dayana. Aunt Rosa was headed to Orlando, since the New York guests had left days ago, which meant Haydee had packed her bags again. She could've stayed with some other relatives, but she didn't feel like making another move.

Aunt Dayana was in the living room, dozing off in front of the TV. Haydee had her bedroom door open, so she could hear people cheering and blowing on horns. Outside, her cousins were near the parking lot, setting off sparklers and firecrackers with the other neighborhood kids. Their popping sounds drifted all the way up to Haydee's windowless room.

Haydee grabbed a mirror off her nightstand, and that small action set off nerve endings in her body since her limbs were still sore from her tumble on the ground. She patted a bumpy red patch of small, shallow scabs on her chin from the assault, but then she stopped since she didn't want any scarring on her face. She was happy enough that her *birthmark*, from being Rafe's punching bag, had disappeared entirely and he hadn't hit her on that spot during the mall attack. Since she hadn't seen Fernando in weeks, there were no more choke marks on her neck. She was looking like her old self. If she didn't have her tattoos, she would have the fresh skin that she had back in her middle school days. Maybe when she was older and saved more money, she'd get laser tattoo removal.

She stretched, got out of bed, and stepped into the hallway. The living room window beckoned her with its open curtain and with a slight limp she walked over to it to look out at the street scene. Her cousins below were aglow with the fireworks around them. She was always at this window, since it provided the best view of the street. Since returning yesterday, she hadn't seen Rafe's car yet. She hoped she would never see it again.

Hugging herself, she longed to be in Maysa's arms. Maysa made her feel loved and normal. Wishing to shed her loneliness, she walked around her sleeping aunt, threw a blanket on her, then went back to her room to put on a sweater. She tiptoed out and gently closed the door behind her. She was weirded out by being alone in the elevator and even jumped when it landed on the lobby, because a tall man with green eyes was waiting there—it was one of her neighbors, who had a strong resemblance to Rafe, with a lady hanging on his arm. He gave her a drunken smile and wished her a happy New Year.

Haydee wanted to rid herself of the lingering fear. Since the attack, she hadn't opened her old phone to check messages on the app, nor had she downloaded that app on her new phone. She hoped that Rafe had moved on to other girls, even though it saddened her to think that he was abusing, manipulating, and using them to make money. She hadn't had the chance to tell him that she only took the money he owed her, but she knew there was no use telling the truth. Rafe was greedy and stuck to his own agenda. Darla was his puppet, following his orders. She didn't know how the two could have a solid relationship. How could Darla share her body with other men when she seemed to be into Rafe? Ever since meeting Maysa, Haydee didn't want anyone else touching her. Darla and Rafe couldn't possibly be in love like she was.

Haydee joined her cousins and their friends. They were all younger, ranging from six to fourteen years old. One little girl handed her a sparkler, and a preteen boy struggled with a lighter until it lit up. Haydee held the sparkler away from her face. It was beautiful, spewing an uneven circle of threaded light. Kids shrieked, laughed, and held conversations. Cars whizzed by on the busy street north of the complex. When Haydee's sparkler died down, she walked to the outer rim of the complex. Every time she saw a dark sports car, her eyes narrowed. No, there was no Rafe.

She turned to the right and saw a figure facing her. It was a slender girl, about her height, whose head was a tight oval, with fabric spilling off her neck. Her form was in the shadows, but that silhouette looked familiar. Haydee's heart pumped fast, her hopes lifting— she had been thinking about her all night, wanting to feel her skin and taste her lips. "Maysa?" Haydee whispered.

The form walked away. Haydee followed, wanting to see who was behind that headscarf. It could only be Maysa. She must be missing her, wanting to be with her on New Year's Day. They could meet in places that were more secluded, not out in the open where they might bump into people they knew, and Rafe was after her, not Maysa. Even though he and Darla had said disgusting things to her, wanting to treat her like meat, Rafe didn't capture girls and force them into prostitution. At first Haydee had been willing, until that type of life felt like a trap to her.

"Wait!" Haydee called out.

The girl walked faster, sprinting across the parking lot that belonged to another condominium. Underneath a streetlight, Haydee could now see that the girl wore a deep purple headscarf. She also wore a brown shirt with jeans. Her tennis shoes were white, the brightest part of the girl's ensemble. As Haydee got closer to her, she sensed that something was wrong. Maysa wouldn't run away. If she did, she would just lead her to somewhere private, but this girl kept running. Even though the headscarf was in the same style Maysa wore hers, letting her know that this girl was Muslim, the girl's figure was fuller than Maysa's. Her butt was rounder, her thighs thicker, and her legs shorter.

"Stop!" Haydee said, anger tainting her voice. She wasn't chasing Maysa, but someone else. Who was this girl who had been spying on her in the shadows? With Rafe and Darla after her, she needed to know who else was watching her.

The girl ran through some bushes, turning her body through a space between shrubberies. When Haydee did the same, her sweater snagged on the thick stems and thorns of bougainvillea. The beautiful fuchsia bracts were bright underneath the street and condo lights, but the plant didn't feel beautiful. Haydee cried out; the thorns were long, scratching her arms and chest through the sweater.

The mystery girl ran to a car, fumbling with a set of keys. The jingle jangle of keys let Haydee know that this girl was nervous from being caught in the act. When she got into her car, Haydee had a good look at her face.

It was that girl from school, Maysa's friend, the one who always sneered, huffed, and puffed with her gigantic nostrils. Haydee recalled the name ... Aamal.

"Don't be following me no more!" Haydee yelled as the car's tires screeched. "Fuck's wrong with you?" The girl sped away.

Haydee was breathing hard from the run. She inspected her sweater, noticing there were a few runs in it from the thorns. "Damn," she muttered. She didn't care about the old sweater. What she cared about was her safety. It seemed like the whole world knew where she lived. What had Aamal been doing there? Did she live around here? Was she visiting someone? Since there were so many buildings in the area, she had seen classmates around here before, but it was weird to see Aamal there. A girl who disapproved of her and caused her girlfriend grief had intruded on one of her private moments with family.

Haydee's breath wouldn't stabilize. She was afraid, because Aamal seemed vindictive and there had been a falling out between her and Maysa after she caught them making out. Aamal would do something like blackmail Maysa or threaten to spread rumors. She pulled out her phone.

Everything alright? she texted Maysa.

Yes, why? Maysa replied.

Haydee bit her lip, wondering if she should let Maysa know about her run-in with Aamal. That might ruin her night, and she didn't want to worry her.

Nothing, Haydee texted.

That was a lie, because it wasn't a good sign that Aamal had popped up in her territory that night. Maysa had known Aamal for years, while Haydee was relatively new to her life. She felt guilty about that, because friendship meant a lot to most people and Haydee had ruined that for Maysa. Although, from her conversations with Maysa, she knew that Aamal had never been a good friend. Aamal didn't want to let things go that easily. This incident signified trouble. What was Aamal up to? Would she be visiting her again? Was it not enough for her to be nasty to Maysa that she had to torment Haydee as well?

Chapter Twenty-Eight

January 1, 2015
12:09 p.m.

Maysa woke up to a surprise text message from Ruhat. **Happy New Year!** She looked at the message closely. It was one of those group messages, sent to everyone on her list. Ruhat was too much of a follower to be friendly with her if Aamal had blackballed her. There was another surprising message after that.
    I miss you. Happy New Year.
This was from Imani. One of her ex-friends actually missed her. She felt a sharp jab in heart, because she also missed Imani. They would laugh the most, tell each other jokes that Aamal and Ruhat didn't get. They shared their lunches, checked each other's answers on classwork … so much that was now all gone since Aamal was the leader. She doubted that Imani was strong enough to pull away from Aamal. Ruhat and Imani were stuck on her, unless they were going to do something rebellious as Maysa had done, although she didn't see herself as rebellious. She was following her heart, and her heart wanted Haydee.

Maysa wondered if she should respond to Imani but decided against it. After clearing her messages and e-mails, Maysa feigned illness. Her coughs and sniffles sounded authentic enough. There was going to be a get-together of several Muslim families that her parents knew from the mosque. It was an hour's drive, so that meant it would be an all-day thing. She would miss it so she could see Haydee for a few hours. Maysa had invited Haydee over to her home. This gave her both an elated and queasy feeling. She caught herself smiling, and at other times she scratched her head, wondering if this was a good idea. She rarely had people visit and this would be the first time her girlfriend would see her home. Would she be a good hostess? Maybe that didn't matter, because the two girls were a good fit for each other despite their differences.

"Don't go out," her father warned.

"I won't," she promised.

"I'll text you every hour to see how you're doing," her mother said.

"I'll be okay," Maysa assured her. "It's just a slight cold, mostly a scratchy throat."

Her father gave her a penetrating look. The night the police had brought her home, he'd been frantic. He'd spoken of the evils of America, how it wasn't a safe place for young women, that anything could have happened, that she shouldn't have been out so late. He'd been furious, yelling and fussing for an hour before he tired and went to bed. The next day he had cooled down, but still always threw that night in her face. The other day she had mentioned going to the drugstore to buy some bath products, and he reminded her again not to be out late, not to talk to strangers, and to stay in well-lit areas. Maysa shriveled whenever he spoke to her like that, as if she were a clueless child.

She watched her parents and Sanaa leave. The car started, pulled out of the driveway, and they were off. She texted Haydee that she should come over. Even if her parents came early or returned because they forgot something, they wouldn't fuss too much if a female classmate was over. She would tell them Haydee needed a copy of a winter packet. They would never think that their sheltered daughter was a lesbian when they had plans for an arranged marriage. Maysa had advised

Haydee to cover herself so that none of her tattoos would show—her parents would look down on that. Maysa brushed her hair, sprayed on perfume, and put on lipstick.

Within fifteen minutes Haydee was there, dressed in dark clothes from the neck down. She even wore gloves. Maysa laughed at that, because Haydee had taken her warning literally. She didn't even want her hand tattoos to be showing.

Maysa closed the front door, and Haydee immediately kissed her. Haydee put her hands underneath Maysa's shirt, so that her gloved hands were roving across her back. The feel of suede on her skin was amazing, ticklish yet sensual. They were hungry for each other—grabbing, pinching, and sucking. Maysa had an out-of-body feeling. They were standing in the living room where her mother knitted, where her father complained and yelled, and where her sister played with her dolls. Maysa even tripped on a doll, but Haydee held her up.

"Let's go to my room," Maysa said.

She felt more comfortable there, because it was her family-free haven. Her parents didn't walk into her room that much. The bed was all hers, with the scent of her own soap and shampoo, and now it would also smell like Haydee.

After they made love, Maysa flipped onto on her stomach so Haydee could give her a back rub. Haydee's hands were tender, squeezing all the tense muscles.

"Have you, have you, um," Haydee stammered. "Have you seen Rafe around since that night?"

"Why? Would he stalk me?"

"I don't think he'll bother us again. He's stupid, but he's business-minded—for a pimp, I mean. He's probably busy with his drugs and women and whatever else he's into."

"I haven't seen him," Maysa mumbled.

Haydee was silent. She bent lower, so that her hair grazed Maysa's back, and she kissed Maysa's spine, from the top to the bottom. Maysa moaned at the feel of Haydee's lips and the brush of her breasts against her back.

When another hour passed, Haydee got up and dressed. Maysa did the same, minding the time. Her parents still had to be at their friend's place, but that didn't stop her from worrying. Her mother had already texted her twice while Haydee was there, and Maysa was quick to respond with, **I'm feeling better**.

The time she spent with Haydee was so limited; it flew by too fast. Maysa felt like she was mostly at fault, because she was always rushing. When she was out, she needed to be home soon so her parents wouldn't question her. Now, she watched the clock, wondering when her parents would come home. Her father was probably in a living room or outdoor patio area, yelling about politics, the horrors of American life, and how difficult his job was. Then his friends were equally loud, while the women all shuffled to their own room or corner, not as loud as the men were.

"You keep looking at the time," Haydee noticed. "I know what that means."

"I'm sorry," Maysa said. "I don't want you to go."

Haydee squeezed her hand and looked around her room. "It's okay. I had a chance to see your home, see your room. This is where you text me, where you think about me, where you dream about me."

"Isn't someone being cocky?" Maysa smiled.

"I'm the same with you. When I'm in my little closet-bedroom, I think about you all the time."

Maysa's eyes misted over. Haydee's eyes also became wet and she wiped away a tear. Maysa pulled Haydee into her arms, her hand riding up her shirt to glide over the warmth of her bare waist.

"I have to tell you something," Haydee said as she walked from the bedroom to the front of the house. She jammed her feet into her sneakers. Then her hand settled on the knob of the front door. "I saw Aamal last night."

"Really? Where?"

"Outside my building."

"Was she bothering you? Why was she there?"

"I don't know."

"Ruhat lives in a condo on your block, so maybe she was visiting and happened to see you."

"It was really weird," Haydee said. "I went after her thinking she was you, but she ran off."

"I hope she's not stalking you," Maysa said. "First Rafe, then Aamal. We must be the most wanted duo in Miami."

"The way she was watching me was creepy."

"Aamal talks big, but I wouldn't worry about her. She's harmless. She's never been in a fight her whole life. She gossips and cuts people down with her words, but she doesn't do much else. She'll never slap anyone or slash their tires or anything like that."

"You reminded me that I'd like to get some wheels soon."

"That would be wonderful!"

"I know. We can go more places together, drive up the coast and have a picnic."

Maysa smiled at those visions of freedom, of being out on the road with her girlfriend. As soon as Haydee left, Maysa felt that aching in her body, from her throat all the way to her stomach. She hadn't wanted

Haydee to leave. She should've stayed an extra hour or two. Maysa stood on her porch, wearing a casual sweat suit with a plain black scarf on her head. The scarf had been on her bed during their lovemaking, scrunched up beneath their bodies. It smelled like Haydee's soapy scent. Palm trees blocked the street view. Maysa went ahead and took her scarf off, burying her face into the fabric. She smiled again, but then her smile wilted when she heard footsteps scraping along the concrete path leading up to the front door. She hastily put the scarf back on, with nips and tucks to the fabric that probably looked sloppy.

Maysa turned to go inside, so she could pretend to be sleeping or not at home. She didn't expect anyone and didn't want neighbors and family friends bothering her. It was too late, though, because the voice cut into the chilly January air.

"Don't go inside," Aamal said. "I need to tell you something."

Maysa turned around to look at the angry face, the perpetual frown, and the flared nose that seemed to look down on everyone and everything. They were the same height, yet Aamal appeared taller than she was.

"What is it and what are you doing here?" Maysa asked.

"Imani and Ruhat are upset that you're not talking to any of us," Aamal said, stepping onto the porch.

"I don't care. You guys unfriended me and you had your conditions."

"Don't be petty. We can friend you again. We're all worried."

"Why are you worried?" Maysa spat. "How can you be worried about someone you don't even care about?"

"That's not true." Aamal's voice hardened. "You're talking about years of friendship, years of sitting together at lunch, in class … going out together."

"Barely—"

"I'm here to tell you something alarming. That girl you're seeing…" Aamal paused dramatically and closed her eyes before continuing. "That girl was a prostitute."

Maysa stilled. How had Aamal found out? Her breath quickened. She wanted Aamal out of her face and out of her life, and she wanted her to leave Haydee alone, too. Haydee's former life as a prostitute was private, not something for others to know, but here was Aamal—a person she was trying to cut from her life—putting the truth out there. If Aamal knew, many others probably did, too. Even though their clique kept to themselves, Aamal sometimes chatted with the yearbook classmates and others who were chummy with her. If she wanted to hurt someone, she'd spread the gossip around.

"I heard it from someone reliable, a classmate of ours," Aamal said. "Think about all the STDs she must have. Don't get involved with someone dirty and trashy like that. If you want to experiment or are curious, I can understand that. It's something that will pass. No one will approve of this and you're doing something risky, but you can stop it. Maysa, I know your parents. Our parents know each other, and we go to the same mosque. Think about all this, how people will talk, how people won't want anything to do with you if this spreads further."

"It'll only spread further if you lifeless, gossiping hens keep talking about it."

"I see you've picked up manners from that girl," Aamal said. "The old Maysa would never talk to me like that."

"Well, this is the new Maysa, and I like who I am very much."

"You should be ashamed. Think about your honor."

"Honor?"

"Yes, your honor, you know … the core of you, your values, the way you present yourself, the way you represent your family and culture. You have none, but me, Imani, and Ruhat want to restore your honor."

Maysa huffed hearing Aamal's little speech. This was all nonsense, because these old-fashioned, traditional notions of honor didn't match who she was in this century and country. She wasn't willing to give up Haydee for her *honor*.

"You don't believe me, but we'll bring that honor back in your life," Aamal said. "We'll pry you away from that girl, make you see her for what she really is. You need us."

"I need Haydee, not you."

"Oh sure, rely on a street slut."

"I'm not going to be threatened by you," Maysa said. "You talk about friendship, but we were never friends. I've never laughed at any of your jokes, itched to talk to you about urgent things, or was dying to go shopping or eat out like friends are supposed to do. I admit I felt protected when I was with you. It was just us Muslim girls. We were tight out of necessity, to feel comfortable, but we never had a true friendship. I don't care about the stares or words any longer. I can join clubs and meet new people. My world will no longer be a small one, because I don't have to listen to every single thing my family says, and I certainly won't have your clique rule over me."

"You weren't saying any of this months ago! You

163

were the one who suggested that after high school we should all move in together, be roommates at college."

"That was a naïve fantasy I had. Now I wouldn't live with any of you. I'd rather chew off my own arm than have any of you as roommates when I see how small-minded you are, and you are a snoop as well. I know you were watching Haydee last night."

"I was out and happened to see her."

"Yeah, right. So you proceeded to watch her in the creepiest manner possible. I know that look you give people. I've seen it when you judged me talking to male classmates, as if I was hot to go to bed with them. You whined about my crackling, nervous voice when I made class presentations. You didn't want me talking to football players for the yearbook, when I was just congratulating them on their wins and interviewing them—I know how dumb you think the jocks are. Well, guess what? Some of them are actually smart. And what were you doing today? Were you camped out at my house? You just happened to be here after Haydee left—don't lie, because you were waiting for her to leave, so you could talk to me. I don't care that you saw her here."

Aamal rolled her eyes, but Maysa wasn't done speaking.

"None of you can make me quit seeing Haydee. So take your ideas of honor and shove it up your asses. You're all cold, loveless, and lifeless. None of you have any real joy in your lives."

"Oh, you'll regret your words," Aamal said, stepping off the porch. On the pebbled walkway, she looked up at Maysa with shiny eyes. "We will have to come up with a plan to make you see that what you're doing is wrong."

"Don't threaten me any longer! Don't talk about

regret! I regret nothing! Get off my family's property!"

She was being loud and didn't care. An elderly woman across the street stuck her head out of a front door. Another neighbor was walking a dog and paused in front of her house. Aamal's nose widened, but she turned away and left. Aamal had parked her car at the end of the street, and she drove off. Maysa sighed and the frown unraveled on her face, her skin becoming smooth again after Aamal left the neighborhood, but at the same time there was a thread of worry winding around her head. What were Aamal and her ex-friends planning to do to *restore her honor*? It was over between them, but Aamal, Imani, and Ruhat didn't want to let go of her.

It was true that people wanted what they couldn't have. She shook her head in confusion, then went inside. She locked the door, pressed her back into it, and closed her eyes. That had to be the most honest moment of her life. It felt good, but scary, to say what was on her mind. Aamal was sure to share her monologue with Ruhat and Imani. She didn't care … for now. Winter break was almost over and she'd be facing them in a few days.

Chapter Twenty-Nine

January 5, 2015
11:44 a.m.

Meet me for lunch, Haydee texted.
Okay, at the concession stand, Maysa replied.
Get me some hot chips before they run out
Fine
Haydee smiled. She never made it to the concession stand on time for the hot chips, which ran out fast. Everyone else wanted that mixture of salt, spice, and crunchiness. Maysa's mid-day class was closer to the cafeteria and concession stand, whereas she had to walk all the way across campus from her computer class. Her stomach growled on the way over. It was cold for a January day in Miami. People wore sweaters and sat in the sun, on either the lawn or any available benches.

No one looked at her. She was glad, because she had something on her that she didn't want anyone to know about. The gun was tucked between an undershirt and her khaki pants. Over that she wore her uniform shirt, the baggiest one she had, and a plaid shirt for this cooler weather. With Rafe, Darla, and even Aamal on her tail, she didn't feel safe. The gun was heavy against her body, and she was afraid that a school official would be on to her, which meant jail time and being kicked out of school. She had known other students, in her past life, who brought guns to school, but it didn't make her feel any better that they had gotten away with it. At any moment, she thought she could be whisked away and arrested. She had too many things going against her, but she had to think of safety for herself and Maysa.

She was almost at the main building. Through a

breezeway she could see people coming to and from the concession stand and the cafeteria. She wanted her hot chips, and she also wanted to see how Maysa was doing. It was the first day back from winter break. How were her ex-friends treating her? Were they giving her a hard time? A few days ago she told Haydee that Aamal had talked to her in a threatening tone. If that girl didn't leave them alone, then Haydee would have to deal with her. Aamal was dense and didn't understand that she was out of Maysa's life. It wasn't that Haydee didn't want Maysa to have friends, but she didn't need friends like that. It would have been wonderful if that clique was accepting of them. Haydee would have welcomed some more people in her life, but that didn't happen.

A girl dashed across the lawn to the walkway where Haydee was. Even though it was cold, she was wearing a school uniform that was too tight for her curves—her school shirt hugged her breasts and stomach and her khaki pants looked like a second skin. She was also tattooed, with dark marks all along her arms.

The stranger stopped in front of Haydee, who paused. The girl had dark eyes, long hair tied into a messy ponytail—and a bruise underneath her left eye. Haydee's mouth opened, but nothing came out. Maybe she was an athlete or had some other excuse for the bruise, but everything about the girl reeked of the life Haydee used to have.

"You Haydee?" the girl asked.

"Yes," she responded. "Who are you?"

"Doesn't matter who I am. Rafe wants to see you. He says you left a bunch of clothes and makeup at his place."

"I don't want them."

"Sure you do. I saw it … nice stuff."

"I don't do that shit anymore. You can have my things if you want."

The girl looked her up and down, all the way from Haydee's dirty sneakers to her hazel eyes. "You'll be back," she said. "Might as well get paid for it instead of giving it away for free. Listen, because this is serious— Rafe said he'll tell your aunt what you've been doing."

"He's not going to blackmail me to return to him," Haydee growled, her voice low and angry. "My aunt won't believe him. Was I on a payroll? Did I give out receipts? He can talk all he wants. It's like I never existed."

"You're a hard one. Well, I tried is all I can say."

"How'd you know where to find me?" Haydee asked.

"Darla said you come here, and so do I. I enrolled today."

"Why bother? Why not drop out?"

The stranger laughed, throwing her head back. "Are you kidding me? I'm off to do business right now."

The girl strutted to the electives building. There had been rumors that people often had sex in a stairwell that was a blind spot away from security cameras; and they also did it in a boys' bathroom in that building. This girl was off to meet a john, or two or three or maybe more.

Haydee walked slower to the concession stand. It upset her that one of Rafe's hoes was in school with her. She doubted that the girl would do anything to her, but just the fact that she was connected to him put her on alert … she could pass along messages and threats. She doubted Rafe would step foot on campus with all the cameras and security monitors around, but what if he picked this girl up from school? At her old school, he sometimes drove Haydee to meetings with johns. What could he do in the parking lot or around the school, though? Haydee touched her waist, where the gun was, but then retracted her hand immediately. She hoped no one had seen the outline of the gun. She hurried toward the hubbub of the main building, where she would join Maysa for lunch.

Chapter Thirty

January 9, 2015
2:10 p.m.

It was hard to stay clear of her former friends since they shared many classes with her. In yearbook class, the first five minutes had been extremely tense. Everyone could sense something was wrong. People looked back and forth between Maysa, who sat by herself, and the ex-friends, who huddled together as they whispered and eyed Maysa. Maysa could understand the quizzical looks she received, because at other times, when she saw friends breaking up, she would also wonder why they kept their distance. People were together one day and apart the next for a variety of reasons.

Imani had a wide-eyed face all day. Ruhat had a beady, accusing look on her face. Aamal's face was neutral, with hooded eyes and a mouth set in a straight line. Whenever a bell rang, Maysa either was first to leave or waited until her ex-friends left so she wouldn't bump into them. Several more months of this until summer. One college had already accepted her and she was waiting to hear back from two others. What if her ex-friends were going to share a campus with her? They had discussed going to the same college—with their fantasies of being roommates forever, or at least until they all had marriages set in stone.

Maysa wore boots, and every time she walked they were loud, nothing like the sound of her usual sneakers. One of her relatives had mailed them to her as a Christmas present, and her mother had urged her to wear them, put them to use instead of hiding them in the closet.

The boots were made of black leather with a thick sole, but they weren't her style. The clacking sound as she walked irritated her, because all she wanted was to avoid attention.

In chemistry class, Maysa sat next to Haydee. It felt good not to be alone and to be near her girlfriend. She hadn't *come out*, but she felt like she had with these three girls knowing about her. There were ten minutes left in class, and the ex-friends turned around to look at her and Haydee. Aamal and Ruhat sneered, while Imani remained wide-eyed. Maysa felt a twinge of discomfort for not talking to Imani.

When the teacher asked them to clean their area, Haydee was the one to get up. She brushed against Aamal, who was at the sink, rinsing off beakers. The two looked at each other directly. Haydee was unafraid and bold. Maysa wished that she could be like that. She had been outspoken lately, but she knew she had to break out of her shell more. She told off Aamal on her porch, and she anticipated other encounters like that one.

While Maysa fixed papers in her folder, she felt someone brush against her back. Then a folded piece of paper appeared on top of her classwork. She looked up, but there were a dozen students out of their seat as they returned lab materials to cupboards and a closet in the back that the teacher had unlocked.

She hadn't received a note in ages. People usually texted each other. Notes had been used in middle school when students didn't have their phones on them or had hit their texting limit. Maysa unfolded the piece of paper, her heart lifting at the message.

Maysa, I meant it when I said I miss you. I'm sorry Aamal is treating you badly. Please meet me in the back alley of the gaming store after school lets out. My older brother is picking me up there, and he can give you a ride if you want. Come alone, because I want to apologize properly and talk about what I did over winter break. I have a Christmas gift that I didn't have a chance to give you: some DVDs, American Hustle and Silver Lining Playbook and a few others. I know how much of a movie person you are. Also, throw this note away after you read it, because I don't want Aamal or Ruhat to notice it if they pass by you or if you leave it behind accidentally.

The note was in print, with Imani's name in cursive on the bottom. Of course Maysa would go. She adored Bradley Cooper's movies. He was her second favorite actor, and she would love to have his movies in her collection. More than that, she wanted to speak to Imani. It would be nice to talk to her one-on-one, without the menacing presence of Aamal and her toady, Ruhat.

She scanned the room, glancing over Aamal and Ruhat so she didn't have to look into their eyes. Students were still milling around and talking, getting their areas cleaned up. In between the students in motion, Maysa caught a glimpse of Imani, who was back in her seat. Maysa nodded, as did Imani.

Maysa crumpled the note and threw it in the closest garbage can. Imani urged her to come alone, and she took it that she didn't want her to tell anyone about this, and that included Haydee. If word were to reach Aamal, she might get mad that Imani was being friendly to her. It seemed enough that Aamal was furious at her, although maybe it was time for the clique to be broken up completely.

Chapter Thirty-One

January 9, 2015
2:20 p.m.

Haydee had seen that Imani had tossed a note at her girlfriend, who then read it and threw it out. Was it a threat, an apology, what? On her way back to her seat, she saw that the note was at the very top of the garbage can, on a heap of balled up paper. She pulled it out, turned into a corner so no one would bother her, and read it.

It seemed harmless enough, so she put it back in the garbage can. It had been a private note, not meant for anyone else but Maysa, so she wasn't going to bother her girlfriend. If Maysa wanted to be friends with this girl, she was no one to judge. Imani seemed like a better person than the other two girls in that clique.

When the bell rang, Maysa and Haydee got up and stood by the door, with everyone else walking past them. Maysa looked around nervously. "Um, I have to go to the plaza two streets over to buy some arts and crafts things for a project."

Haydee maintained a neutral face. "I'll text you later."

"Oh, okay," Maysa said. "I thought you were going to walk home with me or offer to ride with me on the bus."

"No, no, that's okay," Haydee said. "My cousins might need me to help them with their homework, so—"

"Oh, all right. Well, later then."

The two of them walked out of the building together, but then they went their separate ways. Students who drove their own cars headed to the parking lot, others went to the bike rack or the line of buses, and some waited for a parent to pick them up. Haydee sometimes took a public bus, but she also sometimes walked. Today she would walk, going straight home to look at car ad fliers since she was serious about getting her own car. In the distance she caught sight of Maysa crossing the street. After she crossed, she saw Imani, who was wearing an olive-green scarf. A few minutes after Imani crossed the street, Haydee then noticed two other figures waiting to cross, one with her hair covered and the other with frizzy dark hair—Aamal and Ruhat. The gaming store was two blocks away, one plaza over from the one that was directly across the street. Whereas the one closest to the school was very busy, the one with the gaming store was almost empty. Many businesses had closed down around the store.

Haydee's instincts filled her with unease. A pressure built up behind her forehead, her chest constricted, and her throat dried up. In the note, Imani wanted to see Maysa alone. It didn't mention that those two other girls would be there. It could be that all three would apologize, but it could also be an ambush.

She shook her head. She didn't want to be paranoid. Those girls were mean-spirited, but they weren't thugs, and Maysa was a big girl. She needed to handle her ex-friends the way she wanted to, without interference. Still, Haydee didn't feel right seeing all of them cross the street minutes apart. It could be that Aamal and Ruhat were going in the same direction as Imani but were headed somewhere else.

"Whoa," she said aloud. She was so preoccupied with these thoughts that she almost rammed her head into a stop sign. She turned a corner, and it was drastically quieter because she was away from the school crowd.

Only one bicyclist zoomed by her. She walked alongside
the empty football field. Across the street was a park with
pine trees that swayed, their leafy branches seeming to
whisper to each other. She stopped in her tracks, allowing
her instincts to take over. Whether Maysa was going to
get mad at her or not, she had to turn around and go to the
plaza to see what was going on between the clique and
Maysa.

"Hey, you," a voice called out.

A car neared her, its slow, smooth glide behind
her not sounding right when there were no intersections
or driveways close by. Haydee stumbled back when it
was alongside her. It was a black sports car. She panicked
and looked around, wondering which direction she should
take to avoid him.

"Yo!" he called out. "You can't get away from me
this time."

Haydee was ready to run, but a girl rammed into
her—it was the new student, the prostitute that had talked
to her before lunch today. She struggled, but then another
female joined the fray. She saw flashes of Darla's face as
she tried to fight the two of them off. The black car
stopped and there was the metallic shriek of a door
crashing open, then something else … the trunk.

The two girls had their arms wrapped around
Haydee and shoved her, kicking and screaming, into
Rafe's trunk. Her feet were on the ground. Then they
were up as hands lifted, twisted, and molded her body
into the small space. Someone rammed something in her
mouth. Haydee's tongue encountered what felt and tasted
like a dry, musty sock. Then they tied something around
her head to keep it in place. They wrapped her hands with
duct tape. Someone reached into her pocket and took her
phone. All through this, she twisted and tried to fight her

kidnappers, but she couldn't do anything when it was three against one. Haydee thought about the lethal weapon tucked into her pants—Rafe's own gun. No one had checked for that. The weight of it pressed against her hipbone.

The trunk slammed down and Haydee squirmed silently in the dark. Kicking and bucking against the gas can, other items, and the sides of the trunk was useless. The trunk rattled with her movements, but she couldn't set herself free. She was trapped.

Chapter Thirty-Two

January 9, 2015
2:32 p.m.

Maysa went to the plaza across the street from her school. Since her school's parking lot filled up fast, some students parked here, ignoring all the tow-away signs. No one ever towed them, though. She said hi to some classmates. She continued walking to another plaza behind it, and this one was almost empty. There was a medical lab in front, a somewhat busy pizza place, and behind it a row of stores that had been closed for years. Phone numbers and leasing signs were plastered on windows with logos of commercial real estate companies. Next to one of these closed businesses was the gaming store.

The parking lot had cars in the front but none in the back. Maysa walked through this empty portion of the large plaza to reach the gaming store. It was closed, too. She placed her hands against the window to block off reflections and get a good look at what was inside. The place was barren with no activity, the only objects being sawdust and dismantled shelves across the floor. During her freshman year, the place had been packed. Before then, when she was in middle school, she would come in to play arcade games. She'd been into games back then, before movies caught her attention. Maysa wondered about this spot, why Imani had chosen it. The note had said her brother would pick her up here. Maybe he worked in the front of the plaza. She remembered him studying biology in college, so perhaps he worked in the lab.

She went around the store, since Imani's note

directed her to go to the back alley. The alley had a row of back doors and metal garage doors where trucks once came to deliver things. She didn't want to sit on the milk crates strewn across the alley since their plastic looked like it was breaking up. Maysa was uncomfortable walking through this spot. She frowned and hugged herself when she spotted cigarette butts, a used condom, and a syringe. She wanted to leave, turn around and text Imani that she would meet her somewhere else, like the pizza place in the front. This place was too empty. And why the back alley? Was it that horrible for Imani to be seen with her? She could've picked another place, even if it was further away, if she was afraid of Aamal and Ruhat seeing the two together.

When leaves rustled along the ground or rats scurried along trash heaps, Maysa jumped, thinking someone other than Imani was here. Every single sound rattled her.

"Hello."

Maysa turned around and her worry lines smoothed out. She smiled, but Imani didn't smile back. Imani had a dark green scarf on her head, with a brown headband underneath and a jeweled brooch on the front to keep it in place. Imani fiddled with the ends of her scarf and bit her lip. Her nutty skin looked pale in the wintry sunlight. Maysa teared up thinking about the many hours she'd spent with her, both in school and out of it. If only Aamal had been out of the picture the whole time. They would have found each other, Muslim girls sticking together. She wanted to hear Imani's thoughts—did she know Maysa was gay and was she still willing to be her friend?

"Um, hi, Imani."

"Someone was very silent during winter break,"

Imani said.

"I'm sorry, but I didn't know … I just don't know how I stand with you and your friends."

"They were your friends once, too." Imani's eyes were droopy and sad.

"Yeah, they were."

"I'm glad you came."

"Me, too, although I wish I had brought a present with me. I actually had some gifts lined up, but after, um, after everything…"

"You don't need to explain," Imani said. "I don't really have the movies on me, anyway."

"Oh?"

"I don't have any presents for you."

"Did you leave the Bradley Cooper movies at home?" Maysa's voice warbled in confusion. She thought this was the point of this meeting … Imani had gifts for her and they would also have a chance to talk.

"No. I don't have any movies for you at all."

Maysa frowned, then took a step back as long shadows neared them.

From around the corner popped Aamal and Ruhat. Aamal wore a navy blue scarf, with a beige sweater over her uniform. Ruhat was wearing a headscarf in public, which she had never done before. Ruhat only covered herself at the mosque, never outside of it. Aamal wore a twisted smile. Ruhat crossed her arms underneath her chest.

"Not expecting us, huh?" Aamal said.

"Good, because we have something for you," Ruhat added.

"Call it a belated Christmas present."

"Yes, and it's definitely nothing related to Bradley Cooper."

"You're going to pay for not being friends with us anymore."

"And for hanging out with that nasty girl…"

All three of them walked toward her, while Maysa backed away. Her feet crunched on a rotting cardboard box. Taking another step backward, she stumbled when a plastic bag tangled around her ankles.

Chapter Thirty-Three

January 9, 2015
2:37 p.m.

Haydee thought about two things during the car ride—Maysa and the gun. She rolled herself on her back the best she could and stuck her bound hands into her pants. She had to roll up her two shirts, and there was another layer with her tank top. After peeling away those clothes to reveal a bare stomach, she reached for the gun and held it with both hands. She trembled, wondering if in the dark and with her confusion she was pointing it at herself. She felt all the bumps and ridges of the gun to ensure it was pointed outward.

The ragged cloth between her lips made her mouth dry, and she breathed hard through her nose. She let go of the gun—knowing that it was straight ahead of her at eye level—so she could try to pull off the rag around her mouth. The rag was so tight that she couldn't put one single finger underneath it. She lifted her arms all the way up and bent her body forward so she could reach the back of her head. Then she was able to untie the rag and pull the fabric out of her mouth. She coughed and spat out the lint and other particles on her tongue. She wanted water, a huge bottle of it. There were other things to take care of first. She had to get out of here and find Maysa. Right now Rafe, Darla, and the new hoe were nothing more than nuisances, because they weren't important. She had to save her girlfriend. Haydee pressed the safety lever of the gun, the slide of it making her tremble some more.

The car stopped. Her body jostled when the driver braked and cut off the engine. Even though being in the darkness with the movement of the car made her disoriented, Haydee had not lost her sense of time. It was a very short car ride, only a few minutes long. Haydee thought about all the secluded spots around her school— parks, the areas around canals, and lone spots around the river. Rafe probably figured he was going to get what he wanted from her today: his money, her body that he could sell, her dignity, her well-being, her future, everything.

He was wrong. Haydee positioned herself so that her back was against a gas can and other junk that was behind her. She blinked, willing herself not to be blinded by sudden sunlight.

There were voices. She first heard Darla. "What are we gonna do with her?" she asked.

"Rough her up some," he replied. "I want my money. She's also going to work tonight, because this guy named Fernando is begging for her."

"What about her girlfriend?"

"I'm gonna get her, too," Rafe said. "Haydee wasn't like this until that raghead entered the picture."

No! Haydee wanted to squirm and kick some more, but she didn't want to make the car shake. She was busy listening, and she had to be ready to attack.

"But what are we doing here?" another voice joined in. It was the new hoe.

"I can't take her to my place like this," Rafe said. "She's probably pissed and hysterical. She also thinks I owe her some money, but I don't anymore since she stole from me. I took care of her. She did well and lots of guys asked for her. We'll talk some sense to her here. No one is around."

The trunk creaked open and light filtered through leaves and branches. The three of them were there, and the sunlight provided the perfect bull's eye since it was shining the most on Rafe. Haydee did not blink. She did the next thing on her mental list. It happened so fast, with her finger on the trigger… Then her finger moved inward, squeezing it. She could neither smell the gun smoke nor hear the shot because her entire being was focused on hurting him so she could save her girlfriend.

Rafe doubled over. Darla and the new hoe screamed. Haydee sat up, throwing her legs over the rim of the trunk. Rafe was on the ground, clutching his bleeding abdomen. His right hand reached for his hip, and Haydee knew he was reaching for a gun since she had seen him wear a holster on that side of his body. He either had another one or bought one to replace the one she had stolen. She shot him in the torso again; this time a hole appeared in his chest.

Darla and the other girl looked from Rafe to Haydee. They weren't running away, even though Haydee had the gun pointed at them.

He fell and rolled onto his side, blood pooling around him. Underneath an open shirt was a white tank top with blooming red stains stark against the fabric. "Fucking bitch," Rafe croaked.

"Last time he'll call us that," Darla remarked. "We need to get rid of the body."

"Huh?" Haydee gaped.

"Put the gun down," Darla said. "Help us get his body into the trunk. What, you think I really loved him? We're free now! Aren't we, Jen?"

"Yes, free!" the new girl said. "Come on."

Rafe moved around the car, crawling on the ground and trailing blood everywhere. He was trying to make it to the car door, but then he collapsed completely. Even through the dark dirt and spotty grass, the blood was evident. Rafe bled profusely, although Haydee was positive he was dying or dead by now. Darla took a box cutter from the glove compartment and sliced through the tape around Haydee's wrist. She then made a move to lift one of Rafe's arms. Her high-heeled shoes sank into dead leaves and grass. Haydee and Jen wore practical shoes for school, and they had an easier time shoving, pulling, and rolling Rafe over. They lifted his upper body, while Darla worked on his legs until he was in the trunk. This was all surreal for Haydee—the body she was holding had once stood tall and strong and had brought her so much pain— but the survival compartment of her mind took over. The body had to disappear so the authorities wouldn't find it and question her.

"He's barely got a pulse," Darla said after feeling his wrist. "He's a goner."

Haydee blinked back tears. Even though he had tried to destroy her, she couldn't help but think of times when he had been tender and had taken care of her. She pushed those feelings aside so she could think and act fast with the issue of Maysa pressing on her mind. Her new phone with the turquoise cover was sticking out of his back pocket, and Haydee grabbed it before Darla slammed the trunk closed.

Jen pulled a towel from the backseat and they took turns wiping blood off their clothes and skin. The situation sank into Haydee. She had just killed a man. There was no way she was going back to jail, because she couldn't be away from Maysa for days or months. She thought about the footprints she was leaving everywhere. Despite Rafe's body being inside, she needed the car to get to Maysa, because walking and running would take too long when it would only be a few minutes in the car.

"I need a ride," Haydee said. "My friend's in trouble, really bad trouble. I think she's gonna get hurt."

"You'll ride with us and then I'll get rid of the car, the body, and the weapon," Darla said. "It'll be like Rafe never existed."

In the backseat, Jen wiped the gun and box cutter with her sweater to get rid of fingerprints. Darla was in the front driving with Haydee at her side. Here was Darla, Rafe's favorite girlfriend, acting as her accomplice. She never thought the other hoes felt the same way as she did, wanting Rafe out of their lives. Now they were even helping her by giving her a ride, because she had to rescue her girlfriend. Traffic at certain intersections was ridiculous and her heart stopped whenever she saw a police car. Rafe was fading away in their trunk. At least he wasn't moving, since she didn't hear or feel any thumps. She was a time bomb of emotions, the only relief being that she was getting closer to the plaza. She had to get to Maysa before her friends hurt her.

Chapter Thirty-Four

January 9, 2015
2:44 p.m.

Maysa righted herself, kicking the plastic bag away from her. Now all three girls were surrounding her. She looked back and saw that the end of the alleyway was a dead end. She was hoping there was an opening, somewhere she could squeeze through, but there wasn't. She would have to get past these three girls. How could it be that she had spent years being friends with them, but now she was afraid?

"You look scared," Aamal stated. "Why is that? Do you have such a low opinion of us?"

"Don't you trust us?" Imani asked.

No was the correct answer to all of their questions, but Maysa didn't want to anger them. She had to be smooth and soothing and lie if she had to so she could escape. Obviously, Imani had lied in her letter. She'd lured her here for this ambush. What were they going to do? An anti-lesbian intervention, tell her that she was wrong for falling in love with Haydee and that what she was doing was disgusting? The next words out of their mouths proved Maysa right.

"Ever since that girl came here, you haven't been the same," Aamal said.

"We want things back to the way they were," Ruhat added. "We used to all get along, be friends. I want to stick to our college and rooming plans. You and that girl—"

"Haydee—"

"Ruined everything."

"Aamal said she saw the two of you kissing,"

Imani said. "How could you do such a disgusting thing? You're not gay."

"That is against our religion," Ruhat said.

"What would your parents say?"

"Think about your family."

"And us. You're not thinking about us."

The three of them were talking on top of each other. Maysa's head turned this way and that, until she looked through the gap between Ruhat and Aamal. There was freedom past their bodies, where she didn't have to listen to them droning on about what a filthy, treacherous lesbian she was. Their world had fallen apart—their clique was minus one person and that person had done something horrible in their eyes—and they were putting the blame on her.

"You're just confused," Ruhat said.

"Tell us you were experimenting and come back to us," Imani said. "Let's return to the way things were."

"Before that girl, that girl, ughhhhh—" Aamal made a sour face.

"She has a name," Maysa said softly. "Her name is Haydee."

The three quieted down after hearing Maysa's voice. The silence only lasted a few seconds. Maysa surged forward, moving to the right, but then Ruhat blocked her. She moved to the left, and Imani shoved her back.

"We're not in a fucking playground!" Maysa said.

"Oh, the lesbian is teaching you curse words, too," Aamal said. "Hold her down!"

Imani and Ruhat grabbed Maysa's arms. She bucked like a rodeo bull, moving both girls left and right, but they wouldn't let go. Maysa kicked, her heavy boots meeting Ruhat's shins. Ruhat released her, as did Imani.

"Stop!" Maysa screamed. "Help me, someone! I'm in the alley!"

Panicked, she ran to the dead end instead of the opposite direction. The three girls followed. They looked like innocent schoolgirls with their book bags still on them. Maysa also had her book bag, but there was only a notebook and a few folders in it, nothing that she could use as a weapon. Imani and Ruhat stopped a few feet from her. In between them was Aamal, who was the furthest away from her. Instead of a book bag, she had a satchel sitting on her hip. Aamal reached into it and pulled out blue gloves.

"What is that?" Maysa asked. "What are those gloves for?"

Aamal grinned as she slipped the gloves on both hands. Then she reached inside her satchel again and retrieved a bottle. The glass bottle was etched with all sorts of large and small print. It had to be from chemistry class, from the closet that their teacher kept locked. Maysa gasped, because she knew what it was. She thought back to the recent lab that had frightened her so much … the one involving acid.

This could not be happening to her. Her mind froze. She was in the United States of America, a developed country, the best country in the world—although her parents complained about the loose morals and unfair politics, she knew it was the best place to be. Things like this happened in her parents' home country. They did this in Pakistan, mainly to women … this acid throwing. But she was in Miami. How could this happen in Miami?

Aamal opened the bottle and got closer to her. Maysa tried to run again. She shoved Ruhat and Imani. When she reached Aamal, her ex-friend made a move as

if to fling the acid at her, but then changed her mind.
Maysa was moving around too much, and she pulled out
her phone from her pocket, unlocking it. She pressed for
emergency, but her thumb kept hitting the space above it
instead. Ruhat and Imani caught up to her and grabbed
her by both arms. Her phone fell to the ground.

"Keep her still," Aamal said.

Her minions rammed Maysa into a wall, but she
wouldn't stop moving, wouldn't stop fighting. Ruhat
pulled her arm back and shoved her fist into Maysa's
stomach. That took the wind out of her, the pain
spreading through her abdomen. Imani balled up her hand
and rammed it into the middle of her face. These girls had
never fought anyone in their lives, but they hurt her, the
pain in both spots blossoming. Her nose was swelling.

Maysa went down on her knees, viewing the three
of them through blurry eyes. She could also hear them, as
if their voices were penetrating a fog. Her mind wasn't
processing everything because of the pain, but she
understood the gist of things.

"This was meant for your friend, your lesbian slut,
Haydee," Aamal said. "We planned on following her and
throwing this into her face. We know she's the cause of
this rift between us. Yet seeing how you stand up for her
and aren't willing to let her go, you have betrayed us. You
also have lost your honor."

Honor. That was such a big word, especially in
their parents' part of the world where women had acid
thrown on them over issues like adultery, jealousy, and
money. "Imani, help me, please," Maysa rasped. "Don't
do this. You'll be arrested."

"No, we won't," Aamal said. "We'll say that we
were with each other, and I can even get my brother to
say that we were all in his presence rather than in yours.

Your precious girlfriend did this to you. It was a lover's spat. You had a fight. She handled this same bottle on the day of the lab. See, station nine is written on it. That's her lab table. You were lab partners that day."

Their chemistry teacher often labeled things to monitor who used what, and she wanted pairs and trios to use the same equipment and material and be responsible for them. On the side of the bottle, through her fuzzy vision, Maysa could see 9 written large and in permanent marker.

Imani shook her head. Out of the three, only she had tears in her eyes. Ruhat had cold eyes, while Aamal's burned with power. Aamal neared her, the cap off the bottle. Imani and Ruhat grabbed her arms and pressed on her shoulders to keep her down. Maysa made a last minute attempt to fight them off, squirming and trying to get up. Her boots were flat on the ground, but her stomach hurt so much that she couldn't catapult herself up. She needed time to recover from the punches, but she was running out of it. Aamal wasn't going to allow her to recover. She was going to carry out her sick plans to hurt her.

Aamal threw the acid on Maysa's exposed face. There was smoke and the screams of an animal piercing the air. The smoke emanated from her burning skin, while the screams—so disturbing that she didn't recognize them, hadn't ever heard such a loud, painful sound before—were coming through her own lips.

Chapter Thirty-Five

January 9, 2015
2:49 p.m.

The intersection in front of the school was the worst, with red lights lasting for minutes and a snarl of traffic. "Come on, turn green," she muttered.

"I hope everything's okay with your friend." Darla gripped her hands together, as if in prayer. "I'm sorry about all this. You probably thought I hated you or something. I don't."

"And I never hated you," Haydee said. Even though the tension wouldn't leave her body, it felt good to get this off her chest. "I think we all felt the same way, but didn't know how to get out of that lifestyle."

"I'm going to cosmetology school," Jen said.

"I've been thinking about that myself." Darla locked eyes with Jen and the two women nodded at each other.

"It's up ahead!" Haydee said when she saw the plaza. "Thank you for the ride and good luck with everything." She couldn't stay and talk any longer. She didn't even wait for Darla to drive inside the plaza. Since the car was already in the right lane and stopped at a light, she got out, slammed the door, and ran to where a medical lab and an Italian restaurant advertising pizza were. A large pizza pie was on the glass exterior. The front of the plaza was busy, while the back had no cars at all. As soon as she hit that section, she knew something was wrong. Not only was that section empty, but it was dark and gray, with peeling paint and the interiors of stores in shambles behind dusty, dirty glass.

Haydee's legs kept pumping. She continued to run

to the gaming store. She was new to the school, but she wasn't new to the area. When she was younger, all the boys talked about this gaming store before business dried up.

A side stitch slowed her pace. Her stomach cramped from all the running and her calves also ached. The alley's entrance was in view, its gray and black depths setting itself apart from the open spaces of the rest of the plaza. She slowed down and walked to the alley's opening. Her eyes widened and she ran to the stumbling, screaming girl. It was Maysa, smoke coming from her face—her skin was red and bubbling.

"Help!" Maysa screamed. "Help! Someone hellllllp! I can't see! It hurts…"

Haydee grabbed her arm, but then felt something eating at her hand. She pulled her hand away. The small amount of acid stinging her hand was nothing compared to the chemical thrown on her girlfriend's face—undiluted, splashed in close proximity. The trio of girls scurried out of the alley. Ruhat and Imani were running with pained looks on their faces. They had their hands held out, and parts of their skin were discolored.

"It got on me!" Ruhat screamed.

"Water," Imani said. "Let's find water to wash this off."

Aamal was the only one who looked uninjured. She stopped and turned as if to confront her. There was a bottle in her gloved hands.

"No, let's go," Ruhat said. "My skin is … is … is burning!"

"Let's get out of here," Imani gasped.

"What is she doing here?" Ruhat screeched. "You said there would be nobody else here!"

Haydee had surprised the threesome, since they

had no idea she'd snooped and read Imani's letter. Her girlfriend was screaming with her body doubled over, her hands on her face—the acid was burning through layers of skin. She didn't know what to do, how she could undo this or take away Maysa's pain. She pulled out her phone so she could call for help. Aamal neared her, twisting the bottle cap open. Haydee's throat closed off as she panicked, but she acted fast. She surged forward and punched Aamal in the face.

The bottle fell to the ground and rolled away. When it hit a pillar in front of an empty store, it burst open, the caustic contents mixing with pebbles, wrappers, and leaves. Some of these materials sizzled, popped, and frothed in the liquid, the acidic smoke causing Haydee to breathe through her mouth instead of her nose. Aamal held her face, with blood from a broken nose pouring through her fingers. Her angry eyes met Haydee's. Then all three ran off. *Cowards!*

Haydee put a hand on Maysa's back, but her girlfriend shrank away, as if her whole body had become sensitive to any little thing. Haydee was in panic mode— breathing hard and on the verge of tears as she called 911. It was hard to concentrate on the phone call when Maysa was screaming. As a calm male voice soothed her and told her to stay on the line, two young women who wore aprons with logos of the pizza place ran to them. "Oh my God," one of them said. "Her skin is burning! Was there a fire? Let's get her water!"

They hooked their hands through Maysa's armpits, pulled her up, and led her to the pizza place. Maysa was stumbling, about to trip, but the girls held on to her and led the way. Haydee followed, with the 911 operator still talking to her. "We're inside a restaurant, close to where the attack happened," Haydee told the man on the phone.

Customers gaped. Some people stood and backed away in fear. The two women took Maysa into the back, where the sinks where. One of them pushed Maysa by the small of her back so she was leaning over the sink, while another pulled at the faucet spray hose and doused Maysa with it. While she was in that position, Haydee couldn't see her face. She had seen the damage though—the skin melting, the smoke, the redness as the acid ate her flesh.

Haydee couldn't think straight. She had been kidnapped, had killed Rafe, and now this. The operator urged her to tell him what was happening, but she handed her phone to a waiter so she could stand next to Maysa.

One girl was still hosing Maysa's face. Her mouth was spitting out water, which meant her face still worked. The acid hadn't gone through the muscles, although her red, raw skin was in a frightening state. Haydee's chin quivered, but tears didn't fall since there was too much adrenaline in her body. She could only watch, unable to help her girlfriend. Maysa had her hands underneath her chest, catching the water that was falling off her face. Her hands must've been burning as well, because she had covered her face with them in the aftermath of the acid attack. Not too long ago Haydee had gotten to know this face—kissed, caressed, and dreamed of it—and now it was damaged.

Another waitress came by and led Haydee toward the adjacent sink and turned it on. Haydee shook her head. "No, I'm fine," she said. She tried to yank her hand back, but the waitress was insistent.

"Let me wash this off," the young brunette said. She pulled Haydee's hand under the blast of water, which soothed the few blisters she had. Washing the area was only a minor relief in the face of seeing Maysa in so much pain.

There was a lot of noise. People were standing and gawking. Paramedics rushed through the door, and they pulled Maysa away from Haydee and the waitresses. Haydee tried to follow but wasn't allowed in the back. "Sorry, no." One paramedic brushed her away. "We'll be at Miami Memorial if you want to see her."

The police were there. At first Haydee's heart jumped seeing them, because not too long ago she'd shot someone, but her mind separated the two events. She pushed memories of Rafe to the side, because Maysa came first. Still, Haydee was aware of some stray blood spots on her clothes that she hadn't wiped hard enough with Darla and Jen's towel. There was also blood underneath her fingernails. The police didn't seem to be noticing this in the face of what had just happened. The two women who helped were talking to them and they pulled Haydee into the conversation as they all stood outside the restaurant. Haydee let loose with the truth about who the culprits were.

"Three girls from school ran from the alley," Haydee said, giving them their names. "Sorry, I don't know their last names. One of them had a bottle of acid and it fell to the ground. You can see the shards over there."

"The school is still open," a young, female officer said. "We'll send someone there right now. And what is your relationship to Maysa?"

The officers kept saying her name wrong. May-za. My-sa. Haydee stopped correcting them, but did say this: "She's my girlfriend. Those girls committed a hate crime."

Now that Maysa was headed to the hospital and there was no urgent need for Haydee to do something, all the tears she'd been holding back fell freely. Also, she didn't feel like hiding the truth. Once the officers talked to those three bitches, the truth was going to come out, anyway. Haydee had been fantasizing about the day when they both could come out, but the clique and their outrageous acid attack changed everything.

Chapter Thirty-Six

January 9, 2015
5:00 p.m.

"We're taking her into surgery soon," a voice said through the haze. "The damage to her face is severe…"

Many voices surrounded her, but she couldn't make out everything people said. More voices joined in, so she knew her family had arrived. She sensed her mother and sister crying, while her father badgered someone, a doctor or nurse, about whether or not they could fix her face. "Can my daughter's face be fixed?" he asked. "Tell me the truth!"

My face, Maysa thought as someone wheeled her away from the many voices. What about her face? There had been the burning, so intense, like nothing she had ever felt before. Aamal had splashed acid onto her. Her ex-friends were the reason she had screamed like an animal to the point that her throat became raw. She wanted to scream again, even though the drugs through the IV subdued her pain. She wanted to scream because she felt violated, and because she knew something bad was going on with her face. Did she even have one anymore? She pictured a red, puckered mass of flesh on her head minus a distinguishable nose, mouth, and pair of eyes. Was her face a blob after all that burning?

She wanted to be with Haydee. Her love had been the one who saved her, who had come to her rescue. If only she had come a few minutes earlier… Haydee had shown up, which meant that she had tried. If it weren't for her, she would have burned and burned, screaming in that alleyway with her ex-friends holding her down so that no one from the front of the plaza could see her.

She wondered about Haydee's safety. Aamal had that bottle of acid initially to harm Haydee. Had they run off? Were they pursuing Haydee, or were they behind bars? In the haze, Maysa really wanted to know. Her mind replayed the afternoon.

Maysa had kept her eyes closed because of the acid fumes—and the acid may have splashed in her eyes, which would explain why she couldn't see. The damage? She wanted to know about it.

"We're going to put you under," someone said. "You won't feel a thing…"

No one was wheeling her anymore. She was in a warmer room with different voices around her. The hospital odor was both clean and disturbing. Everything smelled like rubbing alcohol, whether the nurses or doctors actually used it or not. Maysa's nostrils weren't covered. Her mouth wasn't covered either, yet she couldn't open it. She imagined that her flesh had melted together, because her whole face felt stiff. She couldn't open her eyes either, but something was over them. She tried to twitch her eyelid but couldn't do so. Did she even have eyelids anymore? She breathed in deeply, but then someone put something over her nose. The drugs knocked her out.

In her dreams, she relived the attack. The clique was throwing punches and chasing her. They were calling her lifestyle *haram*, unclean. Aamal threw the acid onto her face … *splash*, *splash*, *splash*, the liquid droplets sailing onto her face with the fling of Aamal's hand. A plume of smoke erupted from her skin, as if she were a building on fire. The smoke reached the sky. She put her hands on her face and her hands melted. Her handless arms ended at her stubby wrists. She ran, but this time there was no Haydee or restaurant girls to help her. She screamed and cried, the acid eating into her face. She had no eyeballs left, no nose, and no tongue. She fell to the ground, a sack of raw skin and bones.

She wanted to wake up, but couldn't. One nightmare after another plagued her. At one point, she felt doctors and nurses prodding her, but then she went to the land of nightmares again, where she was so alone. No one could visit her in the hospital room since she was recovering from surgery—she heard words like *recovery*, *surgery*, and *no visitors* in the haze—and no one helped her in her dreams.

Then a figure cut into the nightmare. Through the smoke walked Haydee. Haydee lifted her up, put her arms around her, and her flesh grew back. She grew new eyes, a new nose, and a new tongue. Her skin renewed itself. Maysa didn't know what was real and what was a dream anymore. Haydee became the center of her dreams. They were together not physically, but in her mind, and this provided comfort to her on a day that would forever change the way she looked and the way she lived.

Chapter Thirty-Seven

January 9, 2015
5:00 p.m.

No one would let Haydee see Maysa. "Maysa Mazari," she asked one security clerk after another, as if one of them would eventually say yes.

"Are you family?" the last one asked.

"No."

"Sorry, you can't go through."

Other people were handing in ID cards and receiving visitor badges, but not her. Haydee saw three people walk into the lobby. There was a tall, brown man and next to him was a pale woman with a headscarf. They had a little girl with them, Maysa's sister. The security clerk gave them directions to the floor they should go to in the burn center. Even though she had been a witness to the attack, Haydee frowned in disbelief that her girlfriend was in a place for burn victims.

Tired of pacing and sitting, and having people bar her from seeing her girlfriend, Haydee went to a restroom and scrubbed her hands. She took wet towels and wiped off the few spots of blood left on her clothes. When she didn't see any more, the need for coffee hit her. With worries numbing her brain, she drifted to another area of the hospital for a cup of coffee. People with laptops and tablets surrounded her and she asked a man one table over for the Wi-Fi password. She had limited data on her phone, so she logged into the café's network. She went into her browser and looked up *acid attacks*.

Bile rose in her throat as she studied the gruesome pictures. Women had chins melded with necks, as if their faces had melted like candle wax. Some had no eyelids, noses, or ear cartilage. They had been blinded, with opaque eyeballs that could no longer see. Their lips had burned off, so their teeth stuck out. Women had piebald, splotchy skin. She shivered viewing all the females who had acid disfigure them this way. Only a few pictures of men and children were evident. This happened mainly to women in parts of the world like the Middle East and South Asia. There were before and after pictures. These women looked unrecognizable.

Haydee searched acid attacks in Europe and the United States. Things were different for victims in those areas. They had skin grafts and wore pressure masks. They had scars, but they were far less pronounced than the women from poorer countries. The worst case in Europe involved a Belgian woman who had so much acid poured on her that her face was beyond repair, even after she had numerous surgeries. Despite the surgeries, she looked nothing like her former self.

Tears leaked out of Haydee's eyes. No one would let her see Maysa. She thought about texting her, but that wouldn't do anything. Maysa had to be busy with surgery and treatment, and she probably didn't have her phone anyway. She assumed one of those bitches had stolen it before the attack.

Two police officers walked into the café, but Haydee wasn't alarmed. Her girlfriend was on the forefront of her thoughts.

The officers soon left with coffee cups in their hands. Haydee was in a corner, with no one being able to look over her shoulder. She went on all the local news sites.

Man found dead by canal…
High school girl victim of brutal acid attack…
Those were the two biggest news items of the

evening, and Haydee had a connection to both of them. That same sensation she'd felt when she'd placed Rafe's body in the trunk hit her again. This was surreal. She went from doing petty crimes in her gang to being a prostitute, and now she had murdered someone in self-defense, and the girl she loved had been disfigured because of her.

Because of her. Haydee blamed herself for the attack. She should've been there sooner. If she hadn't been a prostitute in the first place, Rafe wouldn't have kidnapped her, so she would've saved Maysa right away since she would've reacted to Imani's letter without anyone blocking her way.

Then there was the issue of their entire relationship. If she hadn't gotten involved with Maysa, her so-called friends wouldn't have done this to her. But who did such things? Who were those girls to tell Maysa what to do and how to live? How could their love be wrong in their eyes? Haydee cried harder. People stared at her and she rushed out of the café. She lingered outside the hospital, wondering which window belonged to Maysa's room. It was getting dark, with the hospital lights appearing brighter as the sun went down. When she was so tired that she felt like passing out she took a bus home, even though home was the last place she wanted to be.

Chapter Thirty-Eight

January 29, 2015
2:10 p.m.

Maysa's parents told her that she must be confused, that the drugs she took through her ordeal must have muddled her mind, and that the girls at school must be spreading vicious gossip. Their daughter could not be gay.

"But I am," Maysa had repeatedly said from her hospital bed.

Her face was no longer covered in bandages and her eyes were open. She was not blind, as she had feared, since the bottom of her face had been burned the most. One doctor had said that forty-five percent of her face had been hit by acid, but in Maysa's point of view that was rounded off to half. The acid had affected half of her face. There were no mirrors in her room—not even in the restrooms of the burn unit—nor had anyone given her a small hand mirror, so she had no idea how she looked. Her face felt heavy and tight, as if she couldn't fully move it. Her hands had also been affected. She knew what her hands looked like—the palms reminded her of pieces of raw steak whenever a nurse changed the dressings, and this was after the skin grafts. The doctors and nurses assured her she just needed time to heal, but she worried she'd always be red, pink, and grotesque—a patchwork of normal skin and acid-affected areas of flesh.

She'd thought her oil burn from weeks ago was bad. That was nothing compared to this. What did her face look like? Curious, she would touch the edges of her face with the fingers of her better hand—the one that hadn't been burned too much—even though she was told not to. She knew she had to look ugly. Her mother would never again suggest an arranged marriage for her. What man would want her in her current state?

Her parents switched from droning on about what other people were saying to asking her if she was comfortable in her hospital bed. While her parents fussed over her injuries and her gayness, she pondered how the acid must have transformed her face. She knew about acid attacks, had seen them on TV, and some distant female relatives had suffered through them. Her mother said two of her cousins had been through such attacks. What if she looked like a monster? She wanted to cry, but her head was buzzing with too many thoughts of the past, present, and future. Then there were her parents' voices invading these thoughts. She wanted to sit in a dark room by herself, with no stimuli, no one to talk to her, and most certainly no one looking at her.

Her mother and father sat next to her bed. Her mother held on to one of her wrists, since her hands were off limits, while her father wore a stern frown.

"You do not know what you are talking about," her father said. "What is this gay business? Why are all the newspapers saying that your friends attacked you because you are gay?"

"Because it's true," Maysa whispered.

She was still weak from the surgeries, anesthesia, and painkillers. The doctor had told her that soon the hospital would discharge her. She would wear a pressure mask to flatten the skin grafts on her face. She might need more surgery because there was the possibility that the skin on top of her jaw was partially fused with her neck, which would cause tightness and lack of mobility. He also told her she was healing well, faster than previous patients, because of her youth and the fact that she had washed off a lot of the acid at the pizza restaurant before arriving. This didn't make her feel better in the least bit. She was deformed ... that's what nurses and doctors were trying to tell her in their nice, smiley manners.

"Let's not talk about unpleasant things," her mother said.

"But everyone is saying my daughter is gay," her father spat.

"Listen, once we marry her off, she will drop this."

"No, I won't," Maysa said.

"Look at how defiant she is!" her father said. "She has done something terrible with this girl. I have seen that girl on the news with all those tattoos. She probably drinks and does drugs. How can she go on air and say that she loves Maysa? It's wrong. She's making all of us look bad."

"Calm down," her mother urged. "The nurses will come in and wonder what's going on."

"Let's come back at another time," her father said. "Maysa cannot think straight. We'll visit tomorrow. I hope you sleep well. We would stay here if we could, but we'll call the hospital to check on you. Your mother will be here early and I'll come after work."

Her mother kissed her forearm, because facial kisses weren't possible. Her father left, but her mother lingered. She opened her purse and left some papers next to Maysa's right hand. Maysa had begged to read the newspaper articles related to her acid attack, so her mother had finally brought them. She wanted to know what was going on in the real world. There was a TV in her room, with limited channels, and she seemed to be in sleep mode or in surgery whenever she was in the mood to watch the news. Also, she didn't have her cell phone. She tended to occupy herself with reading material. She'd been able to walk around the burn center yesterday, but she didn't want to interact with strangers, so her walk had been brief.

She wasn't wearing a *hijab* in the hospital. She missed wearing a scarf on her head, because she was used to it being a part of her wardrobe, part of who she was. Even though she wanted to wear it, she wondered what modesty was in the first place. Her *hijab* hadn't protected her from the worst event in her life. Instead of being attacked by men who couldn't control their impulses, her own kind had attacked her. Her female, Muslim, ex-friends had tried to take everything away from her.

Maysa moved the papers onto her lap with the uninjured tips of her right hand. The narrow stack was in small print, probably because her mother wanted to save paper. Exhausted and with drugs in her system, Maysa brought the first paper to her face, then the other, and the other. Whenever she spotted her senior pictures—the ones she had taken in a professional studio and had ordered a set of—a burning sensation traveled up and down her throat. Those pictures were a reminder of how everything had changed during this last year of school, which was supposed to be a happy one. One of those pictures would be in the yearbook.

She pried her gaze away from those senior shots in which she posed in profile, to the left side, to the right, and facing directly at the camera—her old face was symmetrical and pretty. Instead she focused on the text.

Aamal was the ringleader. Imani had lured her to the attack site, while Ruhat wore a *hijab* because she didn't want anyone recognizing her as she walked to the plaza. The girls had first planned to attack Haydee—the illicit girlfriend of a devout Muslim girl—but then turned on Maysa instead. Aamal had stolen the acid from chemistry class. It was undiluted acid, taken while she was pretending to put things away. Classmates described her as a teacher's pet, someone sweet to adults but who had a mean streak with peers. Their chemistry teacher was horrified, and she was on paid leave pending an investigation on whether or not she followed procedure in handling dangerous chemicals. All three girls were currently in jail and awaiting trial for the assault.

Maysa put the papers down and breathed hard, reminding herself that she didn't have to worry about those three, because they weren't free to attack her, her family, or Haydee. She continued reading. She had been in the hospital for weeks, and outside the hospital there was a media circus regarding her assault. There were pictures of her family's house, her parents, her mother crying, and her father shrugging off a reporter. Then there were the parents of her ex-friends, also crying and evading reporters. She recognized all of them—they had eaten dinner together, went to the mosque together, and visited each other during Ramadan and Eid. They had prayed in the same room, facing Mecca and being devout, but they had raised these monsters who'd disfigured her. Maysa steadied her breathing and went on reading and skimming, devouring this information.

Haydee is dying to contact her and complained that she isn't allowed to visit. She has told several local news reporters that she is in love with Maysa Mazari. Various LGBT charities and organizations are willing to help the couple with medical and living expenses after this hate crime.

Maysa wondered if that was the reason she had a

recent room change. Her new room was much nicer than the one she had been in, with a view of the river and condos around it.

News outlets are calling it a hate crime against homosexuals and blaming Islam's stringent laws for the girls' small-mindedness. The parents of the three perpetrators are in disbelief. They believe Maysa instigated the situation. They claim these actions are out of their daughters' character. They are also looking to sue the school, indicating that a teacher should not be using undiluted acid with students, although advanced high school classes use the substance in laboratory work.

"Yeah, right," Maysa said. "Not innocent and not winning any lawsuit against the school."

She needed to send a message to Haydee. They hadn't communicated since the attack. She put the sheets aside and pressed a button near her bed so that a nurse would come. "Did you need something?" a petite, blonde nurse asked.

"Is my family still out there?" she asked, her lips stiff. She was healing and her face felt fragile during the process, so she tried not to make any sudden movements with it.

"Yes, they are. They're at the nurse's station asking the doctor about your next procedure. Would you like for me to get them?"

"Can I see my little sister, just her alone?"

"I'll ask if that's possible."

A few minutes later Sanaa was in the room. During these visits, Sanaa would be in her room for a brief time, a few minutes, before her parents asked her to sit right outside the hospital room. This was because Sanaa appeared petrified during these visits and also because her parents didn't want her to listen to their questioning of Maysa's gayness. Alone with her sister, she looked at Maysa with wide, frightened eyes and quivering lips. Maysa imagined that she looked like a mummy with her patchwork of grafts. "Sanaa, I need you to do me a favor, and it's a secret. You can't tell Mom or Dad that you're doing this for me."

"What is it?" she asked in a small voice. Her gaze was riveted on her sister's face.

"Get me a pen and paper. I want you to write something for me."

Sanaa stepped out and returned, bringing back a pen and pad of paper with the hospital's logo on both items. Maysa didn't want to write anything herself, because she didn't want to upset her healing hands—and she also feared that any movements would set off a ripple effect of intense pain. She was delicate and unable to do everyday things in her condition. So far, she had yet to hold a pen in her hands during her hospital stay.

"Write this down: *I love you and I miss you. Nothing has changed between you and me.*"

Then she gave Sanaa her e-mail address, her password to it, and Haydee's e-mail address. Haydee had written it on one of her folders once, early in their relationship when they were talking about helping each other with chemistry homework, when what they really wanted was something more.

"I need you to send this e-mail to my friend," Maysa said. "It's very important, or I wouldn't be asking you to do it. Mom doesn't use the computer too much, but I always see you on it."

"Okay. I'll do it when I get home."

"Thank you."

Her sister put the piece of paper in her pocket and left. Maysa placed the stack of news items on her bedside table and focused on seeing Haydee again. She thought about their times together, when her face and hands were smooth, and when her hair had been loose in the privacy of one of their bedrooms. She was carefree and beautiful in Haydee's arms. Now she felt ugly. Would Haydee even love her like this? The newspaper articles said she did, but would she change her mind after seeing her in this state? She didn't know of any young person who wanted to live life like this, or to be with someone in this condition.

An overwhelming swell of despair hit her. She had no friends, couldn't be with her girlfriend, her parents questioned her sexuality, and she was missing school because of her injuries. She might not be able to graduate on time. What about college? There was nothing wrong with her limbs, except for the burns on her hands, so she was mobile, but she didn't want to go out and see people. She feared what she looked like. None of the newspaper articles had a picture of her burned state. No reporters had been in her room, and her parents certainly wouldn't want to document her injuries.

Sanaa had left the paper and pen on the bedside table. The pen had a large cap, with a long and wide metallic clip. She reached over and grabbed the pen, then raised it to her face and peered at her reflection. The clip elongated her uneven, raw, red face. The lower portion of her face, from her nose to her neckline, was a slab of meat fresh from the deli. How could this be her face? During her regular life at home, this was not what she washed in the morning and at night; this wasn't what she dabbed moisturizer on or slathered with lip balm. But this was her face. She grimaced, which made her skin look even worse. Then she threw the pen across the room.

Chapter Thirty-Nine

January 29, 2015
6:24 p.m.

I love you and I miss you. Nothing has changed between you and me.

Haydee looked at the e-mail and blinked. Her face was wet and she wiped at the tears, but they wouldn't stop falling. All of the stress of the past few weeks escaped her. People whispered about her and Maysa at school, and she received stares and questions, but she gave everyone the stink eye and street attitude—all those gestures and the stoic face that she'd learned to have in her past life.

It had been nothing but stress piled on top of more stress. She had nightmares about Rafe, envisioning herself shooting him repeatedly, with the blood splattering and his two whores fleeing instead of helping her escape. She wondered about those two—Darla and the new hoe. She had not seen Jen at school since the shooting and she hadn't seen or heard about Darla. She no longer saw news about Rafe, so he was a non-entity, some lowlife that no family had claimed and no one was crying about. Still, even though Haydee appeared to be in the clear for that, thinking about the shooting sent tremors through her body.

She didn't care what anyone thought about her love life. Aunt Dayana fretted over her and the news surrounding her niece. Reporters had been outside their apartment building, and her aunt urged her to stay inside to avoid them. She'd even cried once, thinking that those girls might have thrown acid on Haydee, too. Aunt Dayana didn't pry about the lesbian angle of all the news stories. It was like she had known all along. Haydee was a tattooed tomboy, only dressing girly during the night job she had dreaded, so maybe it didn't seem like too much of a surprise to anyone. Her classmates were more shocked about Maysa's sexuality than hers.

Haydee reread the brief e-mail message. They must be allowing Maysa to use computers at the hospital, or maybe she had her phone with her. That meant she was getting better. Haydee could imagine what Maysa must look like after those burns—she recalled her initial research and seeing those images on her phone when she had been in the hospital's café after the attack—but those girls at the Italian restaurant had rinsed off the acid and she received treatment right away. Could the damage really be that bad? Even if it was, all Haydee knew was that she wanted to be with Maysa.

Lying on her narrow bed, Haydee caressed her bed sheet with one hand, recalling the times Maysa had visited her. She sniffled, then wiped her phone against her shirt to take off the smudges made from her wet hands.

I hope you are doing better. No one will let me see you. Let's be together when the hospital discharges you.

She pressed *send*, then dropped her phone. She got down on her knees and took out the book that held her rolled up bills. She had started working at Aunt Dayana's laundry place a week ago, when her mind was clear enough to function after that horrible day. She was turning eighteen in a few days, and her girlfriend wouldn't be around to celebrate with her. Now that she was of age, she would open a checking account. She would also buy her own car.

The money would be for her and Maysa. She wanted them to live together. She knew this wouldn't go well with Maysa's parents, but she figured they must know about the two of them because of all the news stories. Haydee had actually opened up to some reporters, because she wanted that clique to be vilified for what they had done. On the one hand, she wanted people to leave her alone, but on the other, she wanted to announce to the world that she loved Maysa, that a hate crime had been committed against her, and that she would do anything to make things better for her. She was also going to be at the trial as a witness.

She opened her phone again and typed another e-mail message.

When can I see you?

Chapter Forty

June 5, 2015
9:13 a.m.

"How could you do this to us?" her mom questioned. "How can you leave us for her?"

Maysa was in her room, her face immobile, although tears were swimming in her eyes, ready to fall. This seemed like the hardest thing to do. The whole year had been hard. Leaving her home hadn't been a possibility last fall, but it was the reality now. In a few hours she would be somewhere else, living with her girlfriend. She opened her mouth, with her lips pressing against the clear plastic mask that encased her face.

"Do you really think you can take care of yourself?" her mom continued. "And live in sin with this *girl*?"

Maysa had refused to give up seeing Haydee, even after her father stopped talking to her. When he drove her back and forth to the hospital, it was out of fatherly obligation, and he didn't speak to her during the car ride. Her mother did most of the talking, and everything out of her mouth came out like hard pellets of confusion and disgust. Maysa stuck with Haydee at school. She also stormed out of her house during weekends to see her, even though her parents tried to stop her, even with her father rushing out to yell at her, with the neighbors looking. Nothing was going to get in her way. Her ex-friends had tried with their bottle of acid, but that hadn't dissuaded her.

Maysa finished packing. When she was done, she had two suitcases and five boxes. Haydee was going to come soon, with one of her relatives who had a pickup truck. Haydee was living alone in her own apartment. It wouldn't be easy starting a new adult life. Maysa's movements slowed down as she thought about it, because there would be no safety net of her parents' support or money, although her medical insurance would be steady. She needed that.

Her mother walked out of the room, but Maysa was sure she would come back again. Her mother was like that—arguing, leaving, then coming back to say something else. Her mother liked to pour salt on wounds, making things worse by dredging up the past, throwing mistakes in her face and making her feel inadequate by comparing her to others. This time it wasn't about her grades or attitude. It was about living with her girlfriend, when she had always wanted to control her daughter by setting up an arranged marriage.

She was hungry but didn't feel like going to the kitchen and bumping into her mother. Her sister was watching cartoons in the living room, since school was over and summer vacation had started. She pulled out a packet of cookies from her purse. To eat comfortably, she had to take off the pressure mask.

The mask was to smooth out the scars, and she had to wear it all day, every day. She only took it off when eating or bathing. Her skin was mostly uniform in color because of the skin grafts, which originated from other parts of her body like her back and butt, although there were ripples and patches of scars. Even though she had wonderful medical care and the girls at the pizza parlor had washed off what they could, she would always look like an acid attack victim with lumps, ripples, and an uneven skin tone. She looked much better than the ones she had seen online, though. When the pressure mask was out of the picture, which would be two years from now, she would look into wearing makeup to smooth out the texture of her skin. She was also wearing snug gloves to flatten the skin on her hands. Her whole life revolved around her burn status with the dressings, ointments, painkillers, and numerous surgeries; even in recovery mode, she had to be mindful of burn victim paraphernalia like the gloves and mask.

The incident and its aftermath was all a reminder of her secret love life with Haydee, which set off Aamal's innate mean-spiritedness to new levels. Of course, Imani and Ruhat had followed her like sheep. Maysa smiled, because she realized she had been the strong one, pulling away from the three of them. Nothing could come between her and Haydee.

She sat on her bed and chewed on the cookies. Her teeth felt loose since the pressure mask was shifting them around. Yesterday she had been to the dentist, who made a mold of her teeth for retainers so her teeth would stop moving. Again, there was the sensation that every part of her life revolved around her injuries, because so many things had changed, and she would have to keeping doing more and more—with endless treatments—to make herself appear as normal as possible.

Maysa looked around her room. She had taken most things off the dresser and walls. Just as she was finishing the cookies, her mother walked in again. She was putting on her *hijab*, which meant she was going to face strangers soon.

"There is some truck in our driveway!" she yelled. "Is that girl coming inside? And you do this when your father is at work? I wish he were here to stop you."

"He can't," Maysa mumbled.

"Of course he can. How can you say such a thing? There was a time when you listened to him."

"Not anymore, Mom," Maysa said, slipping the mask back on and tightening it in the back. She also wrapped her head with a scarf. "This is my life and how I want to live it. I love you both, but you can't tell me what to do."

"What did I do to deserve this from you?" her mother wailed.

Maysa couldn't stand it when her mother was being melodramatic. "They'll only be in here for a few minutes," she said gently. "I'll call you when I get there."

Haydee and a wide, tall cousin came in and didn't talk. They wordlessly picked up the boxes and suitcases. They knew not to say anything with Maysa's mother crying. Even Sanaa looked at everyone with sad eyes, and she didn't say a word.

Maysa hugged her sister. She tried to hug her mother, but her mother put an arm up to block her. That hurt, but she told herself that her mother would get over it. Her parents might never accept that she was gay, but they couldn't deny their own daughter, couldn't forget all the years and happy times, and how they loved her. Maysa blinked away tears and walked out.

The hot sun hit the left side of her face inside the truck. She and Haydee sat in the back, holding hands. Her cousin Oscar had the window down to smoke a cigarette. This normally would bother Maysa—no one in her family smoked and any type of smoke or fire reminded her of the acid attack—but she didn't want to say anything. The cousin had already been too kind with his willingness to spend a morning helping her move.

Despite her time in the hospital and all the obstacles of recovery, Maysa had graduated on time with honors. She went to the graduation ceremony, although her parents had not been in the audience. Her father said he was busy and her mother feared reporters would be there. All those years of pressuring their daughter to have the highest grades, and they weren't there to see the end result.

Haydee's family had been there. They were sweet to her during her first meeting with them, and Aunt Dayana had hugged her. Her ex-friends were noticeably gone. Their trial would be this summer, and Maysa had to be there. It would be the last time she'd see them in person. Even though there had been no reporters, students and their family members had cameras and they had zoomed in on her, probably to send pictures to the press. *Lesbian Pakistani girl, victim of acid attack, graduates without parental support.* She made headlines in her head, although none of them sounded quite right. To her it was more like this: *Girl in love graduates high school and is ready for the next chapter of her life.*

Her new home was fifteen minutes from her old one. Haydee's cousin unloaded his truck and left. Maysa was alone with Haydee in their tiny dwelling. The living room and bedroom were both small, but between the two of them they didn't have too many things.

With her gloved hand, Maysa grabbed Haydee's. Her girlfriend squeezed softly. "You're glowing and beautiful," Haydee said.

Maysa smiled. Even with her scars, people told her that. It wasn't just because of the healing process and how the skin grafts and surgeries were all working for her. Whenever Maysa looked in the mirror, with or without the mask, she noticed a glow around her, because she was with the person she loved.

Chapter Forty-One

June 5, 2015
12:50 p.m.

After the two of them spent a few hours moving furniture and putting things in cabinets, they settled in their bedroom for a nap. Haydee's bed, the one from her old bedroom, was what they had for now. It was a tight fit for Haydee and Maysa, but they cuddled against each other. Despite Maysa's healing accessories, Haydee felt comfortable enough to wrap her arms around her girlfriend.

"I have to tell you something," Haydee said into Maysa's ear. A sliver of flesh at the lobe was gone, while the other ear was undamaged.

"What is it?" Maysa asked.

Haydee was on her side, while Maysa was on her back since that was the most comfortable position when she wore the plastic mask. As Maysa stared at the ceiling, Haydee told her about what had happened that day, before she'd made it to the gaming store. She let loose all the details.

"I killed someone," Haydee said. "I killed Rafe. Does it make me a bad person that I don't feel awfully guilty? I know he was horrible to me and the girls, but I think I should feel something. Are you surprised?"

Maysa turned her head to look at Haydee. She blinked slowly, but the rest of her face didn't move much because of the mask. Haydee willed her to talk and not be mad, shocked, or disgusted. "Yes, I'm surprised," Maysa finally said. "Why didn't you tell me sooner?"

"Your injuries were so serious. I focused on how you were feeling and nothing else. I didn't know when was a good time to mention what happened. Am I a bad person?"

Maysa turned on her side, propping herself up on an elbow. "No, you're not a horrible person," she said. "There's nothing horrible about you. You did what you had to do to survive. Even when you were working for Rafe, it was to survive, not because you were meant to be a prostitute. And that day you needed to live and you were also set on saving me."

"Sometimes when I hear a sharp sound, like thunder or the slam of a door, it's like I'm hearing a gunshot. I also wonder if the two hoes that were with Rafe were true to their words and got rid of the car and weapons. What if they didn't get rid of them properly? Rafe's car might pop out of a river or canal and there might be evidence tying his murder to me." Tears ran down the sides of Haydee's face and Maysa wiped them away. She was wearing pressure gloves, but they felt velvety against Haydee's skin.

"You won't hear that sound again," Maysa assured her. "I don't think anyone's really been looking for Rafe or cares too much about him, and I think those two girls were telling the truth. They wanted him gone as much as you did. Don't feel bad about all this. You're with me. You're cleaning up your life. You're away from all the bad people who've ever hurt you."

"I feel so safe now," Haydee said. "I feel safe being with you in our own home. I'll continue to work and I'd like to go to college. I'll be a late bloomer with all that, because these past few years set me back, but I want to be independent and take care of the both of us."

Chapter Forty-Two

June 5, 2015
1:32 p.m.

Maysa held Haydee, who cried on and off. After having a good cry, she seemed calm. Crying wasn't always a sign of weakness, but just a way for people to let loose their emotions. Maysa couldn't imagine killing anyone. That had to have taken a toll on Haydee's emotions, especially so close to the acid attack. Having those two things happen on the same day must have been terrifying and traumatizing for Haydee.

Neither of them was really in the mood for a nap anymore, although they stayed in bed. Haydee's breath became even.

"I forgot to call my mom," Maysa said. "I told her I'd call once I arrived and it's been hours already." Her purse was on the floor, by the bed, and she reached down to pull the phone out. She called her mother, but it went to voicemail. She tried again ten minutes later, but her mother wouldn't pick up. She then texted her, **I got here safe**. Her mom always called back or texted right away, but not today.

Maysa became rigid. She wanted to cry, but mentally put a plug on her tears. She had cried plenty of times since the attack, and it wasn't pretty or comfortable when tears and snot collected underneath her mask.

"What is it?" Haydee asked, sitting up.

"My mom won't answer my calls or texts."

"Give her time. She loves you. You told me so."

"That's what she says. You know what, I'm not going to feel sad anymore. I have you and I have this home. I feel like no one can hurt me again. I'm not fragile."

"No, you're not," Haydee said. "You've been through a lot and I know for sure that you're a strong person." They smiled at each other. She really didn't have anything to worry about, and her mom even texted her a few minutes later, when Maysa had worried she was receiving the silent treatment. **Good that you moved in, be well**.

Her mom was willing to communicate with her. Maysa had decorating ideas for the apartment, and she had college. She'd apply for campus jobs—maybe work in the college bookstore or one of their offices—there was also the charity money that poured in when people read about the hate crime in the news. There was so much to look forward to. She used to think her clique made her safe, but they ended up endangering her. It was with Haydee that she was secure with herself, their love for each other, and their future together.

The End

www.medeiasharif.com

Evernight Teen ®

www.evernightteen.com

DATE DUE

2/15/18		
GAYLORD		PRINTED IN U.S.A.

CPSIA information can be obtained
at www.ICGtesting.com
Printed in the USA
LVOW07s1618161117
556556LV00001B/93/P

9 781772 338928